STATIC

A QUIET WORLD

Jacqueline Druga

PRESS

PRESS

Published by Vulpine Press in the United Kingdom in 2021

ISBN: 978-1-83919-174-9

www.vulpine-press.com

Also by Jacqueline Druga:

No Man's Land
When Leah and Calvin found out they were expecting, they were over the moon. That day would be one to remember forever... but for more reasons than one. That was the day the world changed. That was the day joy turned to fear. A deadly virus broke out, with many of those infected becoming violent and uncontrollable. And it was spreading fast.

Omnicide
A town practically cut off from the rest of the country, Griffin is always the last to know about everything. Fax is the most reliable method of communication and the local newspaper is the main source of outside information.

When a freak car accident occurs on the outside of town, no one thinks much of it. That is until deer are found sick and covered in an unusual growth, and they lose contact with the next town.

Cut off and isolated from the rest of the world, Griffin is unaware of the threat growing outside the safety of their little town. One that could endanger their entire existence.

ONE
SILENT SCREAM

Event Day Sixteen

I was scared.

Scared to the point my guts twisted and turned. My hand covered my teenage daughter's mouth to silence her scream, while my legs wrapped around her body, pinning her back to my chest to keep her from moving.

She was nearly my size, and the struggle was real.

I was scared not for myself but for my daughter and anyone around.

It was straight out of a nightmare.

My daughter in my hold, I wanted to tell her, 'Baby don't scream, don't move, please don't move.' But I couldn't say a word. I couldn't make a sound.

No one could.

I could see the horror in her eyes through the reflection of the patio doors. If I could see her eyes, could he … see us?

I didn't want him to see her.

1

It was hard enough on him.

He was the reason I held her and kept her from moving forward.

I kept trying to move back, out of sight.

The sliding glass doors were open just an inch from when she tried to rush out. I stopped her in time, silently taking her down to the floor.

There was nothing that could be done.

We were far enough away, I knew that. As long as we stayed in the house.

Soon it would be over.

A blip in time.

He had stolen—food, I believe it was. Nothing more than a can of food. Why didn't he come to us? Why didn't he ask me? We had taken him under our wing. Why he would do that, I never would know. Anyone would have given him food. It wasn't the thievery that he was being punished for, it was for the death he caused.

Stupid. So stupid.

Maybe he wanted the punishment and was done with this life.

We all were.

Still … he was young.

My heart broke for him, the fear he was feeling, the regret.

He wasn't a bad person. He was a good kid. A young man not even old enough to drink.

I didn't like the law, but I understood the punishment. I really did. Hate it or not.

An eye for an eye.

I felt my daughter's tears run over my fingers.

I'm sorry, baby, I'm sorry. Words I would tell her when it was safe.

Until his punishment was served any noise ... any ... could cause a chain reaction.

I held my breath and my daughter tighter. It seemed like it took forever. I couldn't really see him, but I would soon enough.

Then it happened.

The static sound through the speaker of the battery-operated record player, the catch of the needle hitting the vinyl, then the end of some old Bing Crosby song played.

Would you like to swing on a star ... Carry moonbeams home in a jar.

Too eerie.

They liked it that way. A spectacle for all to see.

You'd be better off than you are. Would you ...

It played for all of ten seconds; that was long enough.

A flash of white and blue then almost instantly the flames engulfed him. Like some silent version of the Salem Witch trials, burned at the stake.

A warning for all to see.

The way of the land.

I saw a glimpse of his face through the orange hue of the flames. His mouth was wide open as he screamed and cried in pain.

No sound … they cut his vocal cords. They had to for all of us.

His head dropped forward. He didn't suffer long. My insides gnawed in pain for him and that my child witnessed it.

I hated it.

But it was the way of the world now.

It was how we survived.

Quietly.

THE FLASH

TWO
NOT YET QUIET

Event Day One

My broken dryer saved my life. I didn't know it then, but I learned later.

Things were never easy for me and my husband, Gordan. As a couple we got along great, had for most of our lives. But life ... it tested us.

A lot of times they were, in the scheme of life, small things. Like the dryer that just stopped drying, or the tire blowing out two days before pay day.

He would say to me, "Al, things happen. Just go with it."

I never understood how he could 'go with it.' But I guess I did, too. I just didn't realize it. He had a strong faith; me ... not so much.

In hindsight, a lot of couples would have broken over the big events we faced. And they were bad.

It started with Gordan's father being murdered in a burglary right before our wedding. We lost our second child, our son Nicholas, to RH disease three days after he was born. Our home to a hurricane. Then after we relocated. Gordan got the dream job at a local college, only to lose it when a student accused him of inappropriate conduct. While charges were dropped and the student changed his story, it was too late.

Reputation tarnished beyond repair, and we had to move.

Again.

We lucked out. Gordan got a teaching job at a private school in Missouri. It didn't pay nearly what the college did, but we didn't need much. We lived in a small affordable town and I worked at the local chain pharmacy while our daughter Sofie was in school.

It worked.

For years.

I believed that Carthage, Missouri was our saving grace, because even though we still had bad luck for ten years, it wasn't as bad as it had been for the previous five.

We just had the worst streak of bad luck with things.

The dryer being the exception.

"I can't believe you're making me do this," Sofie complained. "Seriously."

"Oh, stop. Just fold," I told her.

The Dillard family, Jan and Bill, were nice enough to let us use their dryer. Jan worked with me at Walgreens and offered her dryers ... plural. With five kids they needed two dryers. So I washed only what I felt was needed, figuring I'd do the rest at the laundromat, and lugged it over there.

We were going to be at their home anyhow for a Memorial Day slash birthday party for their son, Casey.

I didn't plan on needing a neighbor's dryer or the laundromat for very long. I found a 'pay over time' appliance center, where my credit didn't matter. I just needed to find time to get there.

For the moment, the Dillard Dryer was a godsend.

It took forty-five minutes for both loads to dry and it seemed like even longer to fold.

More so because Sofie complained.

"A lot of this is yours," I told her.

"Everyone is up there at the picnic and we're in this dungeon.'

"It's a basement and be grateful or I would be hanging your underwear out to dry tonight."

She groaned this teenaged ... *uh*.

I laughed. "The faster we fold, the faster we're done. Honestly, it's not like your friends are up there. You were complaining anyhow about coming."

"I would have complained more if I knew I was folding laundry on a holiday."

"Just fold."

"Oh my God, do I have to touch Dad's underwear. I'm pretty sure that's like against the law or something."

I snatched the blue boxers from her hand. "Do the towels."

"Fine."

Sofie wasn't bad, really. She was fun. She made things interesting when she had to peek around the basement. The house was the exact same model as our home. Of course, we lived across the street and a couple doors down. Every house on our street was primarily the same. Three-bedroom or four-bedroom, no frills, older frame houses. No more than two thousand square feet. Unless they did an addition like the Palmer family. Most houses had one or two bedrooms on the second floor, the remaining bedrooms on the first.

Our house was a lot like the Dillard's, with an unfinished old basement. Except they had a pool and we, like the Palmers, had an addition on the side. Ours wasn't as big. A twelve by twelve room we used as a family and computer room. The sliding glass doors faced the street, which I never really liked.

Sofie peeked around the Dillard basement, admiring old toys, procrastinating in helping me fold.

Finally, we finished.

We loaded the laundry into two baskets. Both of which were packed and heavy. Admittedly, I crammed the loads.

We had driven the few houses distance to the Dillard's because of the laundry. We carried them out, loaded them in the car, and drove home.

We were quick about it. Bill was making grilled shrimp and that stuff went fast.

We pretty much just opened the front door, set down the baskets and walked back out. We'd put it away later.

I didn't notice when we pulled into our little driveway all the people on the street. Three or four small groups had gathered and were talking. Looking up and looking around. We were only a block from the main town square—was there a parade coming? It was just odd.

Thinking no more about it, we arrived back at Bill and Jan's and headed to the backyard. The sounds of water splashing and kids laughing carried to us.

Bill and Jan had done wonders with their backyard. I envied it. Gordan sat with Jan at the table by the patio doors. The kids ran about, playing with the garden hose and jumping in the pool. As if swimming wasn't enough.

"Hey, there you guys are," Gordan said. "Took you a while."

"Mom made me fold your underwear," Sofie replied.

"Oh, I did not." I laughed and saw she was walking near the pool. "You don't have a swimsuit on."

"Oh, I'm going to squirt the kids."

"Not full blast." I watched her walk over that's when I noticed Bill wasn't on the barbecue. George our other neighbor was. "Why is Bill not grill master? He's the best at it."

Gordan pointed at the house. "He's trying to find out what happened. You missed it. It was strange."

I thought he was joking. I replied sarcastically, "Oh, I'm sorry we missed it."

"It was kind of scary," Jan added.

11

"For real? We missed something?" My eyes shifted when I heard the kids scream and sure enough, Sofie was standing with that hose by the grill blasting the kids. "Hey! Sof! Not full blast. You'll get George wet." I turned my attention back to Jan and Gordan. "What happened?"

Walter, who we all called Wild Walt, walked over. "We thought a nuclear bomb."

"What?" I asked, shocked.

"It got really bright," Walt explained. "Like a flash or over exposure. But no explosion, no loss of power or phones."

"Was it the sun?" I asked. "Maybe one of those solar flares."

"Something that big," Gordan said, "would have taken out everything with power."

Jan pointed to him. "So says the local science teacher."

"I am. What can I say? And there's no radiation," Gordan said. "So it was a fluke."

I chuckled. "Okay now I'm wondering if you're joking. How ..." I paused again. I heard Sofie laugh loudly when George shrieked about getting wet and the kids giggled. With a huff, I looked at her. "Sofie! Stop!"

She waved her hand at me.

"Seriously, that girl." I returned to my husband. "How would you even know if there was radiation?"

Gordan pointed to Wild Walt.

Wild Walt then reached for the table lifting Sofie's green instant camera. "This thing. Pretty much a miniature of the old polaroid, right?" He then lifted a picture. "Would have spots on it if there was radiation. I took a picture right after."

"How would you know to do that?" I asked him.

"A movie. An old movie. Like really old movie. I thought for sure it was a *Where have all the People Gone?* moment and everyone would be gone or turning to dust right now."

"Where have all the people ..."

"Gone," Walt finished my sentence. "A movie. That was the name. Today ... whatever it was, was just a blink. I'm sure it's explainable."

"It's just so ..." My blood instantly boiled when I heard George scream. In a quick mother's rage, I turned to charge over there. "Damn it, Sof ..."

My eyes widened in horror.

George screamed out. He kept screaming. His arms flailing as his entire midsection was engulfed in orange and blue flames.

It all happened so fast.

The children cried out terrified.

In my shock, I was at a standstill.

My husband's, "Jesus Christ" preceded him charging by me, leaping over toys to get to George thirty feet away. He swiped up the tablecloth from a picnic table in his run.

We all were thinking it. The grill. George was standing awfully close to the grill. It just ignited his shirt.

In the few seconds it took for my husband to get there, Sofie in some sort of instinctual move, turned the hose on George.

The water blasted him and he dropped to the ground as Gordan pushed the grill out of the way.

"Keep the kids back. Keep them back," Walt yelled.

"I'm calling 911!" Jan cried out.

I hurried over.

Gordan was kneeling on the ground by George. The table-cloth was by his leg, unused.

Inching closer, I couldn't help but see the expression on my daughter's face. Eyes wide with a complete look of horror. She gripped the hose tightly in her hand, still aiming it at George, as a few drops of water dribbled out. She trembled out of control.

Then quickly I saw George.

His face and arms were untouched by flames. His neck was black and he didn't move.

"Gordan?" I questioned softly.

Gordan shook his head as he lowered it.

Reaching for Sofie, I grabbed for the hose. "Here baby."

"I killed him, Mommy. I killed him, Mommy," she said fast and in shock, still staring at him.

"Sofie ..."

Her eyes shifted to me. "I killed him, Mommy."

I couldn't comprehend why my fifteen-year-old child would think she killed him. Why she would stand there scared out of her mind, unable to barely breathe.

Why?

Then I looked down at George again and understood why she believed she had caused his death, that she, not the flames were the final blow.

George's entire mid-section was nothing but a gaping hole of mush.

I didn't believe for one second my daughter caused his death, but there undoubtedly was a hole in the exact same spot where she had blasted him with the full force water stream.

THREE
COMFORT FOOD AND QUESTIONS

Basic cooking. That was it for me. I never did anything fancy. I thrived on finding the new frozen complete meals, the type you would just throw in a pot and when I bought myself one of those Instant Pressure cookers, that was the closest I had come to being a chef.

Although to Sofie, Gordan and various neighborhood kids, I had a talent for making the perfect ramen noodles.

I was known as the ramen mom.

When they were hungry I did my ramen trick.

Sad ... ramen

Excited ... ramen.

It was the comfort food and everyone asked me to make it for them. The simple instant noodle recipe but I had a secret for making it perfect every time. Noodles perfect, just enough sauce. When Sofie hid in her room after the failed cookout, and George's death, I knew she had to be hungry.

I made her ramen and a cheese sandwich. Her favorites.

She sat on her bed, knees up in a state of despair.

"Hey," I walked in. "I made you dinner. I know you're not hungry, but can you try to eat?"

Sofie nodded.

I set the plate and bowl on her nightstand and sat on her bed. "Listen, I can't imagine what you are going through. I can't. If you need to talk to someone... me, Dad, anyone, we're here. I can call Pastor Jerry."

"Mom, please, no." She gazed at me through the tops of her eyes. "Not him. I don't want him around me right now."

"Oh my God, is there something you're not telling me?"

"What?"

"I mean, like he isn't trying to ...?"

"What? No. Oh my god. I just don't want to hear his positive, things happen for a reason stuff."

"I get it. I do." I ran my hand over her head. "Try to eat before the noodles get big. Just shoot me a text if you need me and I'll be right up. Okay?"

"Okay."

I leaned in and kissed her on the forehead. "Get some rest. I love you."

I stood from the bed and glanced back at my daughter once more before leaving the room and closing the door behind me.

While I was in there, I felt the vibration of the phone in my back pocket and as I stood in the hall outside her door, I looked at my phone.

I had text messages from Jan.

The state police just left, can you believe that? The first one read.

How is Sofie?

I replied back, *Same. Depressed, not saying much.*

You think she is still blaming herself?

I think so, I responded.

There wasn't an immediate reply and I started walking down the stairs.

Beep. *Poor kid.*

Yeah, I thought, *Poor kid.*

As I reached the living room, I saw Gordan on the couch. Leaning on the arm, while he balanced his tablet on his belly.

"What are you doing?" I asked.

"Oh … just trying to take my mind off of George. Thought I'd look up what happened today. You know, with the bright flash."

"Such the science guy. Did you find anything?"

He shook his head. "Hey, did I smell ramen?"

"Yes, I made some for Sofie."

"I could really use some. Would you mind …?"

"No, not at all."

"Thank you," he said. "It doesn't taste the same when I make it."

"It's fine. Cheese sandwich?"

"That would be great."

I stepped back and then paused when I saw the red welt with a slight purple tinge on his forearm. "What happened to your arm?"

"I guess I got burned today with George. I don't remember it happening; then again, it was a crazy moment."

"Does it hurt?" I asked.

"A little."

"I'll grab some ointment after I make your food."

He thanked me again and I went into the kitchen. It made sense that everyone was hungry. We didn't eat much at all.

I was nearly finished making his food when my phone alerted me to another text.

Again, from Jan.

Hey, it read. *I just emailed you the security footage from the backyard. You really need to watch. Start at two-forty-two.*

I replied back a simple, *okay* not really knowing what to make of her request to watch the footage. What did she need me to see? I hoped whatever it was could convince my daughter she didn't cause George's death. Then again, I really didn't want Sofie to relive that.

Leaving my phone on the counter, I took Gordan his food, placing it on the coffee table.

"I'm gonna be on the laptop. Jan just sent me a text that she emailed me the security footage from the backyard."

"She what?" Gordan looked over his shoulder at me as if the idea of that was revolting.

"She said she …"

"I heard what you said, hon, is she actually at home watching the replay?" he asked.

"I guess so.'

"Why would she even send that to you?"

I shrugged. "She said I needed to see it."

"No one needs to see that again. It was horrifying."

"I know."

"Well, make sure the volume is down. I don't want to hear or see it."

"Neither do I but Jan thinks it's important." I reached over Gordan for his laptop that was on the coffee table. I could have used the family computer, but it was slow and old and videos just didn't play well on it.

I set the laptop on the dining room table and lifted the lid.

Just as I prepared to log on, there was a knock at the door. My eyes went immediately to the screen to see the time. "It's ten at night. Who could that be?"

Gordan stood and peeked out the window. "It's Chief Harmen."

"What is he doing here?"

Gordan shrugged and walked to the door opening it. "Hi, Chief, what's up?"

"Sorry to bother you folks ..." He stepped inside when Gordan opened the door wider.

I always liked Craig Harmen. I remember when he was just a patrolman. Just a neighborhood looking guy. No buff, tough guy appearance about him. Average height, a little pudgy in the middle. He wore his hair in a buzz cut with larger glasses like something from the eighties.

The chief seemed a bit nervous. "I've been talking to people; you know since the George incident."

Gordan nodded. "It was horrible. A horrible accident."

"There were a lot of folks there," the chief said. "Is ... Sofie around?"

"Why?" I asked. "She's resting. She's been traumatized."

"I need to ask her some questions while everything is fresh in her mind."

I chuckled sarcastically. "Do you think it ever will *not* be fresh in her mind?"

"I understand." He lifted his hand. "I just need to talk to her. There were a lot of people at the picnic. A lot of people saying she was pretty harsh with that hose."

"Oh my God, our neighbors are closet assholes," I said. "Who the hell would …?"

"Al, please," Gordan stopped me. "Chief, physically speaking she cannot blast a hole in anyone's gut with a garden hose."

"I'm not saying that. She was quick to aim it at him, though," the chief replied.

I scoffed loudly. "A man was on fire. I can't believe she acted that fast."

"Now, hear me out, Al," the chief said, "without getting upset."

I folded my arms. "Now I'm going to be upset."

"No, just listen," he spoke calmly. "She was all about that hose. Do you think… do you think it's possible…"

"No," I cut him off.

The chief shook his head. "Do you think it's possible that maybe she was joking, started a fire—"

"No."

"Started a fire, maybe threw a match, it got—"

"No," I cut him off again.

He continued. "And that's why she was so ready with the hose."

"No."

"Just tossing it out there. Her and the Baynes boy did have that out-of-control campfire last fall."

"Oh my God," I gasped. "Really, that was last year at the scouts' picnic. Big difference in campfire and lighting a man on fire."

"Chief, really," Gordan spoke nearly as calm as the chief. "My daughter didn't do this."

"Can you just let me talk to her or bring her to the station?" he asked.

"No," I replied. "Absolutely not."

"Al …" he said my name.

"No."

"Yes," Sofie's voice sadly spoke up.

We all turned and looked. My daughter stood on the bottom of the stairs.

"I'll go with you, Chief," Sofie said. "You can ask me anything you want. I killed him."

FOUR
DISCOVERY

Teenagers do dumb things. Usually, it's the curiosity or feeling of invincibility that causes it.

Everyone, at one point in their teenage life does something stupid.

Everyone.

It's the nature of the beast. Dumb things. But confessing to a murder usually wasn't one of them.

Sofie poured out her guilt, sobbing in that hyperventilating way. She purged everything in her. She truly believed she killed George with the garden hose.

The chief just kind of stared at her across the table. Me and Gordan sat on both sides of Sofie.

I kept telling her, "Sofie, honey, stop talking until Daddy and I get a lawyer."

"Oh, stop, Al," the chief said. "That's not necessary."

"I killed him. I saw the fire, I squeezed the handle and the water blasted through him," Sofie sobbed.

"Sofie," the chief spoke calmly. "It anatomically isn't possible."

She nodded quickly. "It is. It was like the moment the force of the water hit him it pushed it right through. I watched it go right through."

Chief Harmen ran his hand over his buzzed hair. "Okay, let's say that happened."

"It did," Sofie replied.

"Did you light him on fire?"

"What!" Sofie shook her head. "No. No I didn't. I was playing with the kids. He yelled because water splashed his phone. I never ever lit a match. I learned my lesson last year."

"Okay." I stood. "We're done."

I was grateful she didn't confess to lighting poor George on fire. Admittedly, a tiny bit of me was afraid of that. But I didn't see how that would be. My daughter wasn't a bad kid. Sassy at times, yes, but never bad or in trouble.

"Sit down," the chief said. "We're not done."

"She said she didn't light him on fire."

"I still killed him, Mommy." She looked at me.

"Oh, stop. You did no such thing."

Gordan glanced at me. "Al, please … don't downplay what she is feeling."

"That is the most ridiculous thing I have ever heard," I said.

"I have to agree," said the chief. "Just let's finish her statement and you guys can go."

"Not much of a statement," I replied. "Pretty much she is saying the same thing."

I could tell by the look on the chief's face he was getting irritated with me.

"Aren't you gonna lock me up?" Sofie asked.

The chief shook his head. "No. Even if you did kill him, it was an accident and it wasn't malicious. We'll know more when the medical examiner gives his report."

"Really?" I asked. "I mean, the man died from fire."

"He had a hole in his torso," the chief said.

"I did that," said Sofie.

I ignored my daughter's admission of guilt again and said, "The fire was really hot."

"Not hot enough to melt his insides," the chief snapped.

"And you think a teenage girl throwing a match at him would?" I quipped.

Gordan spoke up. "But gas would."

"Oh, wow, gee, thanks," I said.

"The medical examiner will tell us if gas was used," the chief replied.

"How would she suddenly get gasoline?" I asked.

Gordan shook his head. "No, you're missing my point. Abdominal gas."

Both the chief and I immediately looked at him, while Sofie let out a typical teenage, "Ew."

"It's a known fact," Gordan continued, "that abdominal gas has caused fireballs and explosions during surgery."

I lifted my hand. "Okay, I understand that. The body is cut open …"

"Not always," Gordan said. "It happens with laser surgery.'

25

"Still the body is opened," I argued. "I mean I can see ... maybe ... maybe if George had a six pack of abs. But the only six pack he had was the one he carried and George was big. That abdominal gas has a lot of fat to get through. Good try science guy."

"Just trying to figure it out." Gordan shrugged.

"I'm sure the ME will give us answers," the chief said. "As for now, let's finish, have her sign her statement and you folks can go home. It's been a long day."

He wasn't exaggerating, it was. It was after midnight, we were still at the police station, and I never put all that laundry away. We finally left there just before one in the morning.

When we got home, I gave Sofie some Benadryl to help her relax. It took a good half hour to start working even a little. While she lay in her bed, I put away the laundry. I contemplated letting it go until the next day, but I was having anxiety as well and thought that would clear my mind some.

By the time I finished the clothes, cleaned the kitchen, and made a sandwich an hour and a half had passed. Gordan had passed out with his tablet in his hands and I removed it, placing it on the nightstand and connecting it to the charger.

Still not ready to sleep, I poured some wine and walked to the laptop that still sat on the dining room table.

Looking at the footage probably wouldn't do anything to help calm me, but I was curious.

Jan was anxious for me to see it. So much so she had sent four text messages asking if I watched it yet, reiterating the time stamp I had to focus on.

Gulping more than sipping my wine, I opened the email and downloaded the footage.

It would play faster and smoother if it were on my hard drive.

I opened it, not expecting much and a little nervous about what I would see.

The wide-angle lens on the outdoor camera gave the left and right sides a bending effect. George was in the middle at the grill. My daughter a few feet from him with that hose.

I made the video full screen to get a better look, leaned in, and moved the curser to a few seconds before where Jan wanted me to see.

Sure enough, at two minutes and forty-two seconds, I jumped back with an, "Oh my god." I reversed it even farther back.

I watched George scream at my daughter, probably about his phone. Then again, at that time stamp, I gasped. But the gasping didn't stop there.

"Oh, shit. Oh, shit. What the hell?"

I wanted to immediately wake Gordan, but he wasn't the one that needed to see it. I knew Gordan kept the flash drives and externals in the top drawer of the credenza. I made my way there, grabbed one, and connected it to the laptop.

The drive opened a folder, it was Christmas pictures from years earlier. I hurriedly copied the footage to the drive, ejected it, finished my wine, grabbed my keys, and left. It didn't matter what time it was, I knew I had to share that footage.

It was imperative.

FIVE
TUMMY TUCK

The Carthage Police Department was a big, square single-story building with its own parking lot.

When I pulled in, it seemed that every squad car was retired for the night.

It was a lot calmer than it was earlier.

The single spotlight was lit above the double door entrance. I parked close to that door. But when I pulled the handle to go inside, it was locked.

"For real?" I said to myself. "It's a police station. Why are they closed?" I leaned to the door, trying to peer inside. "Hello!" I called out, then I knocked.

Nothing.

I knocked again.

Finally, I saw one of the officers, Jenkins, walk to the door. He held an apple in his hand. But didn't open the door.

He said something but it was muffled.

"What?" I asked, pulling the handle.

He pointed. "You're supposed to hit the buzzer. Look at the sign."

I shifted my eyes to the small sign that read, 'When door is locked, ring buzzer.' I looked for the buzzer, I finally saw it off to the side.

"Oh!" I nodded. "I didn't see it, thanks."

"Press the buzzer."

At first I thought he was being absurd, then I thought, *what if he couldn't open the door if I didn't press the buzzer?*

Giving a thumbs-up, I side stepped to the buzzer and pressed it, fully expecting the door to open. But when I looked, he was gone.

"Can I help you?" his voice came through the small intercom.

"Are you not gonna open the door?"

"We're closed."

"You're a police station," I said. "I need to speak to the chief.

"He's not here it's three in the morning."

"Then I'll go to his house," I said.

"What is wrong with you, Al?" he asked. "Is this an emergency?"

"Yes. Someone is dead."

"Shit." Within seconds he was at the door opening it. "I'm sorry," he said. "I didn't know it was urgent. Why didn't you call 911?"

"We did."

"Huh?"

"Oh, yeah, we did." I stepped inside.

"What are you doing here?" he asked.

"I need to show something vital to the chief."

"Who died, Al?"

"George."

"That was twelve hours ago."

"Yeah, but I just saw this." I held up the drive. "He needs to see this. My daughter is under investigation for murder."

"It's not really murder, it's involuntary manslaughter."

I huffed. "Whatever it is, he needs to see this.'

"Can it wait until the morning?" Jenkins asked.

"No. It cannot. Now either he comes in or I go to his house and knock on the door until he answers."

"Hold on. Stay put. I'll call him."

"Thank you."

Jenkins reached behind me, latched the door, and walked away.

I took a seat in the hall and could hear him on the phone. Within a few minutes he came back.

"He'll be here," Jenkins said. "Just hang tight."

"Thank you. I appreciate it."

Jenkins didn't stick around, he left me there in the waiting area. That was fine with me. I was right near the front door so I would see the chief as soon as he walked in.

"What's going on, Al?" the chief asked.

I was engrossed in my phone and looked up. "How did I miss you coming in?"

"I came in the back. What's going on?"

"I have something to show you."

"Come to my office."

I stood and followed him through the station, down a hall and to his office.

"I hope this is important." He turned on the lights and walked to his desk. "I was making love to my wife."

"Oh, now, come on, that's not a visual I need."

"Too bad. You dragged me out at three in the morning."

"What people our age have sex at three in the morning?" I asked. "Really."

"If that is an honest question, I feel bad for Gordan. Anyhow ... What's up?" He sat down behind his desk.

"This." I handed him the drive. "There's a video on there. Ignore the Christmas folder. It's the security footage from today or yesterday."

"Jan's?" he asked. "Al, I have it."

"Have you watched it?"

"Not yet."

"Watch it."

The chief proceeded to plug in the drive. "Okay I see the Christmas pictures. What file am I looking for?"

I walked around his desk and pointed over his shoulder. "This one. Skip the first ten seconds."

"Have you been drinking?"

"Why?"

"I smell it."

"Well, then, yes."

"Did you drive here?"

"What does that have to do with anything?" I asked.

"Drinking and driving is against the law."

"No." I shook my head. "Being over the legal limit and driving is against the law. I had wine so it doesn't count."

"Doesn't count?" he blasted.

"One glass. Watch the video. It shows exactly how George caught fire. Now, we don't have to wait for the medical examiner."

The chief clicked the keyboard and the video started playing.

"I said skip the first ..."

"Shh," he hushed me and leaned forward.

"Don't blink, you'll miss it," I told him.

I watched the video with him, standing over the chief's shoulder.

George yelled at Sofie, pointing at her, then wiped his phone on his shirt. Sofie hunched and stepped a few feet from him.

The video then showed George lifting the lid to the grill, waving away the smoke before he stepped a couple feet off to the side.

"See nowhere near, Sofie," I said.

"He stepped away from the grill. How ... Whoa." The chief jolted back. "What the hell just happened?'

"Watch it again."

The chief rewound the footage. "Let me slow it down."

"Can you do that?"

"Yes."

"Wow, you're tech savvy."

"It's a police program." He clicked a few keys then played it again.

Slowly George waved away the smoke, then looked down to his phone. In slow motion, I saw something I missed. He glanced over his shoulder, then moved over with his phone.

"Bet that's his mistress texting him," I said.

"Could be," the chief spoke softly, eyes peeled to the screen.

George kept that phone close, in fact, it rested on his belly as he secretly read or sent a text. But the message didn't go through because with a quick flash of white, the phone exploded and George's entire midsection was quickly encompassed in flames.

Keeping it slow, the chief let it play through.

George stumbled back to the grill screaming. When he did, Sofie turned around, hesitated a split second and blasted him with the hose.

The video clearly showed the water hitting him and as if that garden hose had the force of a fire hose. The stream blasted straight through his body, pushing everything out the back and into the wall of the house.

"Holy shit." The chief stopped the video and leaned back. "The phone exploded."

"Yep. And … it happens a lot. I had time to Google it when I was waiting on you. So you see my daughter didn't light him on fire."

"I see that."

"Although honestly," I said. "He was alive and screaming when she hit him with that hose."

"I saw that too. But Al, if a simple garden hose shot straight through him, she just pushed the inevitable. Something caused those insides to melt instantly. That's nine seconds from explosion to dropping."

"The phone," I suggested.

The chief shook his head. "The phone didn't do that to his insides. Something else did," he said. "We just need to find out what."

SIX
MIDNIGHT OIL

When I finally got around to messaging Jan, she responded back right away. Poor thing was probably sitting around just waiting to know what I thought.

I told her I watched it, was shocked, immediately went to the police, and was still at the station.

Jan messaged she was putting on some coffee, pouring it in the carafe and would be reading in bed, waiting for me.

It wasn't necessary and I told her to feel free to go to sleep. If I saw she was up when I got home, I'd be over.

Chief Harmen truly was in shock over it all. He kept watching it in disbelief, even calling Jenkins in to view it.

After watching it several times and listening to them, I actually wanted to know what the medical examiner thought.

I had been there longer than I anticipated and it was time to go home. I really did want to stop at Jan's, even if it meant drinking coffee and not falling asleep until late morning.

"At least," the chief said, "we can give some answers to George's wife about what happened, even before the M.E. gives us something."

"Who knows," added Jenkins. "Maybe she can sue the phone company."

The chief pointed. "I remember some guy on the news sued the phone manufacturer."

"You aren't telling his wife about the mistress?" I asked.

"No. Not that we know he was talking to a mistress," the chief replied, "but I won't mention about the secretive way he used his phone."

"What is up with that?" Jenkins asked. "I mean, how is the guy this big ... or was this big Casanova? I've been on the force only five years and it's at least twice a year he has a mistress getting him in trouble."

I replied, "He's a nice guy ... was."

The chief nodded. "He was two years older than me in school and it was the same thing. Gigolo George they called him. Captain of the football team, debate team, and match club. He got all the girls from different cliques. Still was nice."

"Yeah," Jenkins added. "He was. Never said a mean thing. I used to feel so bad for him when we'd get called to his house because his wife was beating him. Oh, shit." He snapped his finger. "The last time I was there his wife said she hoped he burned in hell the next time it happened."

"Hmm," the chief. "I guess she didn't mean burn in the Dillard's backyard."

"Alright," I said and stood. "On that I'm going to go. Before I do, you guys hear anything about the weird thing today? What it was? What caused it?"

The chief looked at me curiously. "What weird thing?"

"Some flash. Bright light." I shrugged.

"I missed it. Maybe I was down in records. What time did it happen?"

"I guess about two," I answered.

"Then for sure I was in records. I didn't see it."

"I did," Jenkins said. "It was like the sun got brighter or someone took a picture with a long bright flash."

"Walt said," I interjected, "he thought a nuke went off."

Jenkins laughed. "Oh, it wasn't that bad. What did you think?'

"I was doing laundry and I missed it," I replied. "And I'm gonna go. Let me know if you find anything out."

It was still dark when I left, and would still be for a little longer. It wasn't a long drive back to my street, actually just three blocks.

I could see Jan's house at the end of the street as I slowed down to pull into the driveway.

There was a light in the second-story bedroom window. Which told me she was still awake. It was a soft light and because of that, I debated whether just to go to my house. But since I knew Bill's mother had taken the children because of the tragedy at the house, I wouldn't wake anybody if I went down there.

I parked the car and headed the few houses to hers.

As I drew closer to her house, the light in that second-story room window grew bright. Exceptionally bright orange and white. It scared me at first, I wasn't expecting that. It then dimmed. It dimmed so much it looked like a candle during a power outage instead of a lamp.

My first thought wasn't that something was wrong, it was what the heck was she doing? I walked up to her front door. A blue hue came from the living room window, probably the television, and I could see a hint of the kitchen light. So I walked around the back, and tried the patio doors. They were unlocked. I paused there, flashing back to the afternoon, George's death. Everyone screaming.

Before opening them, I peeked through the patio door. I could see Bill reclined back in his chair, feet up with some old seventies western playing.

Quietly I slid the door open, creeping in like a prowler. The sound of Bill's light rhythmic snoring carried to me. I expected a smell of coffee, since her red carafe was right there with two cups on the counter, but instead I smelled a slight hint of smoke. I thought maybe she put the empty pot back on the burner. But that wasn't it.

The coffee maker was off.

I poured myself a cup of coffee, after all, she had prepared it, and I made my way to the stairs. Four steps up, that burning smell was stronger. It was a strange smell, like sour smoke, something I had never smelled before.

I wondered if Jan was burning a strange, scented candle. Something like, 'outdoor life.' I would have to tell her it didn't smell all that good.

At the top of the stairs, the smell was even more predominant. As I turned to my right and took a few steps, I noticed her bedroom door was partially ajar. It was dark with just the slightest hint of light, probably that damn candle.

I was going to leave, turn around and go, but I kept thinking. She was exhausted, if that candle was burning, perhaps that wasn't a good idea. I'd feel guilty if something went wrong.

My plan was to go in, blow it out, leave, and call her in the morning.

Placing my hand flush on the door, I pushed on it gently trying not to make a sound and wake her.

The door opened wide enough for me to not only slip in, but to see it wasn't a candle.

My body went instantly into a terrified mode. I shook from head to toe. I was so horrified, my hands had no control and the mug toppled from my grip.

I couldn't breathe.

I couldn't even scream.

My God, what happened?

SEVEN
WHAT IS AND WHAT IS NOT

"911 What is your emergency?"

How did I get to that point? How did I get to where I was able to not only grab my phone, but I dialed those three numbers and hit 'send'?

It was a blur.

Hearing the female operator ask that question just sent me into another phase. I wanted to respond, I wanted to say what was happening. But I couldn't. The only thing the operator heard was my gasping, aching, breath as I tried too hard to find the words.

Phone clenched in my hand and pressed hard to my ear, I slid down to the floor, pressing my back against the door frame of Jan's bedroom.

I shifted my eyes to Bill who was on his knees in the bedroom. The moans and cries he made were like none I have ever heard.

Pain, suffering, and heartache rolled into one, crying out over and over.

The operator had to hear him, she had to.

"911, caller what is your emergency?"

At first, I was frozen in horror when I stepped into that bedroom. Then I screamed. I screamed loud and long and wanted to run.

When I spun to leave, I ran right into Bill. He must have heard my cry and charged up the stairs.

Then he walked into the bedroom and the cries he made began.

I heard my heartbeat, my breathing, I had to get it together.

"What is your emergency?"

"She ... she ... oh, God. Please, she's dead. She's dead," I sobbed out. "There's no help, she's dead."

"Ma'am, calm down and tell me what is going on?"

They were trained to try to keep a situation under control, but there was nothing to control in that bedroom.

Sheer panic and horror emanated from both Bill and me.

"Ma'am, where are you? Can you give me an address?"

"One ... One ... Seven ... Six ... Oak." I closed my eyes. "Seven ... Five. Seven five Oak."

Was that it? Was that her address or mine?

I don't recall what the operator said other than she was sending out help. She asked me questions, I couldn't answer.

What I found I wasn't expecting.

It was unexplainable.

No smoke, yet there had been a fire.

I knew as I peered into Jan's room that bright exploding light was what had killed her. The damage was done.

All that remained of my friend were her feet and part of her arm. In fact, her unharmed hand still clutched her e-reader.

When I walked in there was no smoke filling room, yet there was a glow. A small glow that a flame would cause.

It came from what appeared to be nothing more than a pile of burning embers on the bed. Smoldering and glowing.

The flowered quilt was mostly untouched. Only her body was destroyed as if a flash fire just decided to take her.

Calling 911 was automatic, but it was useless. It wasn't an emergency situation, there was no saving her … Jan was gone.

I didn't want to stay anywhere near the bedroom. Now that I knew what caused the smell, I was sick to my stomach. I just wanted to keep screaming and run, but I couldn't leave Bill alone there.

Inching my way out, I stayed in the hall, on the floor, but near the bedroom.

I didn't hear the sirens, but I heard the cars outside, then the voices. It was moments before they entered the house.

"Jan! Bill!" the chief called out.

Bill let out this aching scream and footsteps charged up the stairs.

Chief Harmen was first and stared at me with confusion. "What happened?"

I only looked up.

"Alana, what happened?"

Bill, again, cried out and Harmen rushed into the bedroom.

"Oh, Jesus Christ," I heard him gasp. "Jenkins." The chief stepped to the door of the room.

"Yeah, Chief."

"Get the fire department here. Non-emergency and tell the paramedics hang tight down there."

Jenkins nodded and looked into the room. "Oh my God is that …?"

"Yep."

"I'll take care of it, what about him?" Jenkins referred to Bill.

"You know what? On second thought, get one of the paramedics to come on up with him. Check him out."

"Yes, sir."

Jenkins hurried by me and down the stairs.

"Al." The chief crouched down to speak to me. "What happened? Come on, tell me."

"She … I …"

"Al, I really need you to tell me what happened, okay? Please. Let's start. Why were you here?"

"We … were supposed to have coffee. Talk about George. The video."

He nodded. "I see. And you came in …"

"I saw it."

"You saw her burning?"

I shook my head. "No, I was walking to the house. I saw the light get really bright and then fade."

"So you could see the fire?"

"I guess that's what it was. I don't know. It was bright and then it wasn't."

43

"And you came up here?" he asked. "Because of that." He lifted his eyes upward and watched as the paramedic walked by with Jenkins and into the room.

"No. I ... thought she was awake," I answered. "Playing with a light or something. I grabbed a coffee. When I came up I could smell something. I thought it was a candle. Then I looked in."

"Where was Bill?"

"He was downstairs sleeping. He came up when I screamed."

"When was this? There are no flames. There's no fire now."

"There were no flames when I came up. A few minutes before I called 911."

"No flames at all?"

I shook my head. "Just ... smoldering." My own words, hearing me say them caused me to choke up.

"Doesn't make sense. It had to have happened a while ago." The chief stood.

"No. No." I stood as well. "I texted her. I was texting her from the station. Remember you got irritated with me."

"Chief." Jenkins poked his head out the door. "We have a problem."

The chief went in the room, and I peeked in. He spoke in a near whisper to Jenkins but kept looking over at Bill who was with the paramedic. It was only a moment and the chief came back out.

"Al, did you speak to her personally?" he asked.

"Text."

"So you didn't hear her voice."

"What ... no. It was text."

"You can't be certain it was her."

"It was her. Why wouldn't it be?" I asked, confused.

"I know you're tired and haven't been to bed yet. I need you to come down to the station to make a statement. You know, while it's fresh on your mind."

"I didn't do anything."

"I know." He sighed heavily. "Bill ... Bill has burns on his hands and arms."

My hand immediately shot to my mouth. "No." I shook my head. "There has to be a mistake."

"He has burns, Al."

"He was sleeping. He was sleeping when it happened. I saw ... I saw the brightness."

Just as I was about to respond, I heard Bill.

He cried. "No. No. What are you doing? Come on, Jenkins. What the fuck!"

The chief looked over his shoulder, then to me. "Just head to the station."

He walked to the stairs and waited.

Jenkins came out of the bedroom with Bill. His wrists were cuffed behind his back and he struggled to stop when he saw me.

"Al, tell them," he said, nearly pleading. "Please tell them I didn't do this. Tell them."

"I will," I muttered. "I will. I know."

"I didn't do this ..." he sobbed as he was pulled and led to the stairs. "I swear to God I didn't do this. Tell them."

He repeated those words as they took him away.

Before he went down the stairs I saw his arms and hands. Clearly they were burned. The red scalding marks went from his fingers to his elbows.

I knew in my heart Bill didn't do it.

He couldn't.

He loved his wife.

There had to be another explanation. There had to be.

EIGHT
DEFY AND DENY

They had taken Bill to the hospital for treatment, while I sat in the waiting room of the police station waiting to be questioned.

At first I was so upset. Anxious and nervous, traumatized over what I had seen.

I needed to be evaluated so I could get some sort of sedative. That would have to wait and would have to be something I sought on my own.

More than likely I would just do my home anxiety remedy and take some Benadryl.

Then I saw the medical examiner, Cody Dogan. A young man who had lived in Carthage since he was in first grade. His family moved to town and his father became one of the local physicians. They had lived in New York for a few years after immigrating from Turkey. Mrs. Dogan hated the big city and I don't really know how they decided on our small town, but I was glad they did.

Cody saw me at the station. He was on his way to the 'crime scene,' he said hello and asked how I was.

When I told him I was upset, he ran to his car and handed me a blue flask. A small one.

"Have some of this," he said. "It's brandy. I bring it with me when I have to go to my parents."

I smiled. He made me laugh and I gratefully took the flask, promising to return it.

The brandy helped immensely.

I didn't even think anyone under the age of seventy, or not in Maine, drank brandy.

It was still too early to call Gordan and let him know what was going on. I wondered if he even noticed I wasn't home. He would soon enough. In two hours he would be getting up for work.

I hoped to be home by then.

"Al," the chief called my name from his office. "Want to come in?"

I slowly stood, then walked to his office.

He closed the door.

"Chief, this is ridiculous," I said. "Bill didn't pull a burning bed on Jan. Why would he do such a thing?"

"How well do you know Bill and Jan?" he asked as he sat behind his desk.

"I think pretty well."

"Did you know that Bill has been having an affair with Helen of Helen's Treats in Morgan Heights?"

"What? No."

He nodded.

"How do you know?"

"Well, one of the domestic calls involved her. We have a slew of domestic dispute and abuse calls."

"Bill wouldn't hit Jan."

"No it was Jan hitting Bill."

"One time ..."

"Many," he said. "Mostly when they were out of their Friday night dates. Bill was abused."

"Oh my God. What is it with the women in this town abusing their husbands?"

"The Burning Bed is not so far-fetched now, is it?"

"Stop," I said. "He didn't do it. I know he didn't do it. Chief he was sound asleep when I walked in. Out like a light."

"Eight-five percent of Jan's body was reduced to ash. Do you know how long a body has to burn to be reduced to ash?"

I shook my head.

"Two to three hours. Doctor Dogan said it probably only took two with Jan. Bill had enough time to make a boloney sandwich, have a beer, and pass out before you got there."

"I talked to her."

"Texted."

"I texted her in that time frame. She replied."

"Bill replied," the chief said.

"I saw that bright light."

"I don't know what that was. The Marvin house across the street has a camera that picks up their house. They're getting me the footage and I'll look."

49

"Oh my God." I sat back and grabbed the flask.

"What the hell are you doing?"

"Having a drink. It's been a bad night."

The chief grumbled.

"He didn't do it. I know you say he did, but I just... the sounds he made, the despair. No." I shook my head and drank more of the flask. "You're wrong, Chief. Bill didn't kill her."

"I'd be more apt to believe that if Bill didn't have the burns on his hands and arms."

"Maybe he got them from George," I suggested.

"He wasn't anywhere near George. You know it."

"Can I go home?" I asked. "Please. I'm tired. Gordan and Sofie will be up soon."

"Will you come back down as soon as you get up?"

"I promise." I took another hit of the flask.

"I'll hold you to it," he said. "Come back, finish your statement, sign it, and pick up your car."

"Pick up my car?" I asked. "Why?"

He pointed to the flask.

"Oh, yeah. But it's only a couple blocks, I'll be fine."

Chief just shook his head.

I felt fine, too emotional to feel the effects of the alcohol, but I agreed and after a few minutes, one of his officers drove me home.

With the cool night air, and the silence in the squad car for the few minutes' drive, I actually started to feel slightly light-headed. It could have been emotions more than booze.

50

I thanked the officer and walked into the house. The dining room light was still on and the house had that quiet sleeping feel to it.

After grabbing a bottle of water from the kitchen I went upstairs.

I peeked in on Sofie, she was sound asleep. She would be getting up in an hour's time. Gordan as well. I didn't want to wake him when I walked in. The room was dark, and I used the hall light as my guide.

My plan was to slip into bed and hope to pass out. I didn't want to wake my husband. But the moment I saw him, I felt my heart break and I needed to just hear him tell me everything was going to be alright.

Inching to the bed, I jumped when he spoke, scaring me.

"Are you just coming to bed?"

A tiny whimper escaped me and I wanted to break down.

"Al?" He sat up, turning on the light. "Honey, what's wrong?"

I couldn't even speak. I knew the moment I did I would start crying and wouldn't be able to stop. I felt strong before I saw him, but at that moment I didn't.

Immediately, I crawled into bed and into his arms.

"Al, honey, what is it? What happened?"

My eyes were closed tight, taking in the security of his embrace.

"Al?"

"Oh God, Gordan. You won't believe what ..." I stopped when I opened my eyes and looked down to his arm that draped over me. I lost all train of thought and could only stare at his forearm.

A few hours earlier there was one small burn. Now, blisters and burns covered his entire forearm.

Just like Bill.

NINE
IT ALL CHANGES

Before finally falling asleep, I spent a good hour telling Gordan all about what happened and crying in my husband's arms. Feeling weak, emotional, and like a puppy that just needed to be cradled.

That wasn't me.

I never was that weak ... ever.

But seeing Jan's remains, knowing what happened to her, crushed my being.

Sofie was about as understandable as a one-way track teenager could be.

What happened to my traumatized daughter? I actually contemplated letting her stay home from school, but she came to the bedroom, dressed and ready to go.

"Are we going to school, Dad, or are we not going?"

I wiped my eyes and looked over at her. "Are you feeling alright to go?"

"Yeah. Sure."

"Maybe we should all stay home," Gordan suggested.

"No. Go. School is almost over. I just need to sleep."

"Dad?" Sofie called for him.

"I'll be right down," he said then looked at me. "Are you sure?"

I nodded. "I have to go to the police station anyhow."

"Do you think he did it?" Gordan asked. "You said he had burns."

"So do you."

"Yeah, but, Al, I grabbed for George. Bill didn't."

"I know."

"He was having that affair," Gordan said.

"How do you know?"

"Everyone knows."

"Did you know about the abuse?"

Gordan nodded. "Yep. Maybe he just had enough."

"They have five kids, Gordy."

"I know. But you know, when enough is enough, maybe he snapped."

"No. No." I shook my head. "Bill didn't do it. He was too upset. No one can fake what he did."

"Then what other reason is there?" he asked.

"I don't know."

Gordan leaned down to me and kissed me on the forehead. "Try to rest. Text me when you get up. Okay?"

"Okay."

He looked once more to me before he left, then walked out the bedroom, closing the door.

Before I got under the covers, I plugged in my phone and sent a text to the chief letting him know I was going to sleep a couple hours and head in.

I set my alarm, but I knew I wouldn't need it. I was right.

I had the most horrific dream. All I saw was fire, I didn't know who was burning. Undoubtedly it was because two of my friends met their end by fire in one day.

The details of the dream were sketchy, but it left an emotional impact.

Two hours of sleep wasn't enough, but I woke up on my own. My eyes were puffy and irritated. I felt like I had a sinus infection but I knew it was from crying.

The chief hadn't replied to my text. Not that I expected one.

I made a cup of coffee and hopped in the shower hoping it would make me feel better.

It didn't.

Finally, I left the house and realized my car was still at the police station. The walk would do me good. There was a strange feeling about the day. It felt empty and quiet, and reminded me of the first day of school feeling when suddenly everyone wasn't out and about.

I sipped my coffee as I walked. Turning the corner on the main street, that was when I saw it in the sky.

A trail of smoke, thick and brown. It sent a chill up my spine. Had something happened on a plane? I made a mental note to ask the chief about it.

Only one car passed me on the street; it was way too quiet. No police officers hung outside the station. Squad cars were parked out front.

Before I stepped in, I sent a message to Gordan letting him know I was in the station. He would be taking lunch soon.

I really started to worry when I walked inside and saw no one at the front desk. Just as I was about to holler out "Hello" I saw them all. Ann, the secretary that had been with the department for thirty years, the chief, and six other officers all stood around a desk looking down to a computer.

As I stepped closer I caught the chief's eye. He looked at me and gave me one of those 'upward nods' of acknowledgement.

"Do you want me to wait in your office?" I asked quietly. I figured they were all looking at some police video.

"No need," the chief replied.

"What? Okay. Why?"

When I asked that, everyone looked at me as if I were interrupting or blocking them from hearing.

"There's a lot going on right now," the chief replied. "Al, have you ... have you not turned on the television or been online?"

"No." I shook my head. "I knew something was going on. It's way too quiet out there. What's happening? Was there a terror attack?"

"We don't know. They're still trying to figure it out. But it's bad, Al," he said. "It's really bad."

TEN
WHAT NOW?

A part of me just wanted to run. Get in my car, drive to the school and grab my child. But for what reason?

Are you watching the news? my text message to Gordan read.

Everyone is.

It was shocking.

Everyone gathered around a computer monitor watching the news report.

"The FAA has grounded all flights at this time," the news reporter said. "The loss of fourteen planes this morning due to unexplained explosions onboard is just devastating."

Hearing that was incomprehensible. To think terrorists could just plan something so big. All those families that lost loves ones.

What was going on in the world?

"Alright, folks, back to work," the chief said. "We are going to have a lot of scared folks out there, so let's keep an eye out."

One of his officers shook his head as he grabbed the keys. "What is with all the fires and explosions? Yesterday George Ross and Jan Dillard."

Ann, the secretary spoke up. "Jan was murdered."

"Yeah, but George wasn't," the officer said. "Neither was Carl Frazer."

"What happened to Carl?" Ann asked.

"He was filling up his truck. The pump exploded."

Ann gasped. "Jesus."

"I know."

I listened to the back and forth between them as the officer and others made their way out.

I wanted more than anything to slip behind the desk and keep watching the news, but I knew I could do that at home.

"No statement, Chief?" I asked.

"Not today. Bill's still in the hospital. Just too much going on."

I nodded. "I understand. Can I have my keys so I can go home? I want to watch the news."

"I'll get them."

"Did you hear anything else?" I asked. "I mean, are they saying where the planes were? Were they bombs that caused them to explode?"

The chief shrugged, but another voice spoke from behind.

"It wasn't bombs," he said.

The chief looked beyond me and I turned around.

Cody Dogan stood there. "It wasn't bombs. It was the people."

The chief stepped toward him. "What the hell are you talking about?"

"I'd like to know," Ann said. "I mean are you saying the people on all fourteen flights caused the planes to explode."

Cody nodded. "The fire in the main cabin grew too intense."

I shook my head. "I'm confused. The people on the planes started a fire?"

Cody nodded. "Not on purpose though. There was no bomb. No terrorist. Just like George's phone didn't explode and Bill Dillard didn't burn his wife."

"How did it happen?" the chief asked.

"It was self-igniting," Cody explained. "I started researching this morning. It's not just here or up in the sky, it's everywhere. So many cases, you wouldn't believe. The news doesn't know, not yet, they will. I talked to a lot of other medical examiners. Our theory is pretty solid. They just don't know how to tell people."

The chief held up his hand. "Tell people what? Self-igniting. People are just bursting into flames?"

"It's not that simple. It's a process," Cody explained. "A change in the body that is already happening, and something causes it to just finish. Burn. Explode." Cody leaned on desk to sit down. "It's a lot to take in. It's hard to explain."

I looked to my right when I heard the rolling sound.

Ann scooted her chair over. "Try Doctor Dogan."

"Okay." He took a second and thought. "The body consists of atoms, mainly oxygen, nitrogen, hydrogen, carbon, right? Well, within these atoms are subatomic particles. Protons, neutrons, electrons. Following me?"

Everyone nodded.

"When the event happened, it charged these subatomic particles in the nucleus of each cell in our body. The charged particles can and will cause mini explosions within the cells. There are thirty-seven trillion cells in the body. A few here and there exploding …" He shrugged. "Nothing. No problem. A spot of a million, you have issues. A few hundred million all exploding with the right antagonist, right conditions such as body gases, you have ignition in the body. George's insides melted like this …" He snapped his finger. "He was mush within a second, that heat was so intense. But his phone didn't start the fire, the static or current from the phone was the spark."

"Jan's e-reader," I said.

Cody nodded. "Exactly. It was the spark. It was all she needed."

The chief stuttered some trying to make heads or tails out of what Cody was saying. "Okay are you saying right now, our bodies are charged explosives waiting for the right thing to ignite us?"

"Yes," Cody replied. "The event caused it. Like Hulk and the gamma rays."

"Hold on," Ann spoke up. "You keep talking about an event. What event?'

"Yesterday afternoon. There was a solar event," Cody said. "It lasted about three minutes and that's what did it. Anyone out in the flash will be hit faster, those, say, who were exposed through a window or car a little slower, but damage done to everyone exposed."

"Everyone exposed. And we know this how?" the chief asked. "How do we know someone's body was charged?"

"Like I said it's a process. They'll show signs already. Like ..." He moved to Ann. "Can I see your arms, your legs, or ..." He extended his hand to her.

"What? No." She reached and smacked him.

Cody was fast, grabbing her hand when she did. "See." He pointed. "See these marks." He indicated to the four purple and red marks on her wrists. "Burns. Her cells exploded here. A process. What happened in Jan's body, what happened in George's was like blowing up a balloon, it fills and fills until it pops."

Ann slowly retracted her hand. "And it's happening in me," she said sadly.

Cody nodded.

Instantly I got sick to my stomach because my mind went immediately to Gordan and the burns on his arms. "Will they get worse?" I asked. "The burns."

"Yes," Cody replied.

The chief asked, "Even with no pin to pop the proverbial balloon? What would happen?"

"One of two things," Cody answered. "Without the proverbial pin the balloon would expand and pop ..."

"Meaning the body will burn itself out and ignite on its own," the chief said. "So, everyone exposed is doomed."

"Not necessarily," Cody stated. "The other scenario would be without any more inflation, the balloon would eventually decrease. Meaning without any stimulus, the cells would still burn but slowly and eventually regenerate. Slow enough not to be fatal. Because the more stimulus there is, the faster they burn. It's a chain reaction. The more cells that explode at once, the more chance of self ignition."

It was so confusing, I brought my hands to my head and groaned. "This cannot be happening. This can't."

"Alright." The chief lifted his hand again. "If I am understanding you correctly, if you're exposed, it's not a death sentence as long as you don't do anything to agitate those cells. Is there a way to do that?"

"Yes, there is," Cody replied. "You remove all stimuli. Stimulus meaning, static, electric, noise, anything that causes a vibration or charge. If we want to save the people that were exposed, then we have to do one thing," he said. "Go quiet and go dark."

THE BURN

ELEVEN
CONSPIRACY MAN

In the after moments of Dr. Cody Dogan's revelation, everyone was in awe, asking questions, concerned.

That all quickly changed.

"Why don't we just leave it to the experts?" Ann said. "You cut up bodies."

"Yeah, I do," Cody scoffed, and laughed. "I would think I know more than most people considering I play with people's insides."

The chief cringed. "Oh, stop. We don't need to hear that."

"Wrong word choice." Cody held up his hand apologetically. "Ann, what do you think happened to your wrist then? What is that mark?"

"It could be anything. I'm seventy-six years old, I could have burned it on a stove and forgot," she replied. "We're not saying you aren't smart. You're just not a science guy. Why don't we ask Mr. Cross, he's the science guy."

Again, Cody laughed. "He's a science teacher." He then looked at me. "No offense. I know he's your husband."

"It's okay."

"No one is knocking you, Cody," the chief said. "But the news is saying nothing about this."

"Fine. Fine." He threw up his hands. "All of you can ignite. I'm gonna be fine and watch it happen."

Ann cocked back. "Well, you don't have to be so nasty about it."

Cody said no more, spun on his heels, and stormed out.

After a quick "Excuse me" I hurried and followed. "Doctor Dogan," I called to him. "Wait."

"I'm not in the mood to be made fun of or demeaned."

"I'm not," I said. "I believe you. I do. It makes sense to me."

"Thank you. Do you have any burns or marks?"

I shook my head. "No. I wasn't exposed to it."

"Good. Then if I need your help, you'll be able to."

"Sure."

"Thank you."

Cody gave me one of those 'arm squeezes' and walked to his car.

I needed to go home. But at that moment, standing there, all I could think of was my mother.

With the events of the day before, George and Jan dying, I hadn't called her.

Even though Cody put it in my head that cell phones could trigger the reaction, I felt safe in calling her because she had her phone on the table next to her and just reached over to hit speaker.

I called her.

"Hey, Mom. What ... what are you doing?"

"Oh, Al, is that you?"

"Yeah, it's me. What are you doing?"

"What am I doing?'

"Yeah, what are you doing?"

"Watching the news. Did you see what these goddamn terrorists did?"

"I did. Mom ..."

"You didn't come over yesterday," she said. "You were supposed to come over and do your laundry."

"No, I never said that."

"You did. You said your dryer was broken."

"But, I didn't say I was coming over," I told her. "Mom, how are you?"

"I'm fine."

"Did you by chance see the flash yesterday?"

"The flash?" she asked.

"Yeah, the flash."

"Oh, I don't watch that show."

"No, Mom. Yesterday afternoon," I said. "The sun got really bright and it looked like a flash."

"What the hell are you talking about?"

"Did you see the bright flash?"

"Like a nuclear bomb?"

"Yes."

"Oh my God, did the terrorists set off a nuke?"

"No, it just looked like one. So you didn't see it?" I asked. "Were you outside?"

"Al, what the hell is with all these questions? No. I was in the house. It was the Price is Right marathon. They were showing old episodes. I didn't see it. Did you?"

"No. Mom, do you have any burns on you?"

"My hand when I touched the air fryer. You have to be careful taking hot dogs out of the air fryer."

"Are you sure it's from the air fryer?"

"What the hell else would it be from?" my mother quipped.

"Nothing. I'm sorry."

"Are you alright?"

"Yeah, I'm fine."

And I was. I was happy to talk to her and hear that she was alright. I knew chances were she wasn't outside, but Cody said that people indoors ran a risk of exposure, too. That did worry me.

My mother lived alone and with all that was going on, I just didn't want her by herself. I wanted my mother with us. It took a lot of convincing and pulling the grandmother card, telling her Sofie needed her, but she finally agreed. Even though she was only a few miles from us, I had to figure out a way to safely get her to our home.

Even though my husband was a high school science teacher, he was still one of the smartest people I knew.

If anyone could come up with a solution, he could. When he got home, I would explain Cody's theory to him. I was certain Gordan would find it fascinating.

I was wrong.

"Are you kidding me?" Gordan asked, nearly laughing. "He's whacked."

"No, listen, Cody said ..."

"He's whacked."

"He's a doctor."

"Doesn't make him any less insane. He's always been insane."

"What do you mean?" I asked.

"Come on, remember all that shit he started about an alien invasion in Jefferson?" Gordan asked.

"No."

"He went before the medical review board twice."

"How do you know all this?" I asked.

"I'm a teacher, I hear all the gossip."

"Well he still has his license so the board didn't find anything. Gordan ... Gordan it makes sense," I said.

"Take a second, Al, and really listen. The sun did something to our bodies making our own cells mini sticks of dynamite? And suddenly, suddenly mind you while using the phone or an electrical device, we're going to instantly explode."

"Stop," I said. "It's not that simple."

"Yeah, it is because it isn't happening. It's not scientifically possible," he argued.

"Then explain the burns on your arms."

"I was helping George."

"There weren't that many yesterday," I said.

"We didn't see them."

"What about Bill's burns?"

"Al! He killed his wife. Set her on fire in the bed."

"And the fourteen planes."

"Oh my God," he groaned. "Watch the news. Terror attacks."

"Then what happened yesterday?" I asked. "What happened with the sun?"

"I don't know. I'm still figuring that out."

"Well, when you have it Mr. Science Guy, make sure you alert the media."

"Don't be like that."

I gave up. I seldom argued with him about anything, but he was adamant it wasn't what Cody said.

"Okay. Fine." I turned and lifted my keys.

"Where are you going?"

"To get my mother." I walked to the door. "And by the way. She's staying indefinitely." I made sure I slammed that door when I left.

Still, I was perplexed. Before I put my mother in the car, I really needed to figure out how to do it without the car setting off some sort of deadly chain reaction.

I had a temporary solution. We really had to go only three miles. Of course, my mother didn't understand it.

"Do I smell?" she asked from the back seat.

"No."

"Then why did you put dryer sheets all over me? Good Lord, Al."

"Leave them on, Mom." I glanced in the review mirror.

"I think it's because you think I smell. That's why you have dryer sheets sticking out of me everywhere, and I'm in the back seat."

"I promise you. You don't smell, if you did, I would tell you."

"Is that husband of yours home?"

"Yes."

She grumbled. "He drives me nuts. Thinks he knows everything. I wouldn't doubt if the dryer sheets were his doing."

"They might be." I pulled up to the front of the house and was surprised to see Cody standing out front.

"What's going on?" my mom asked. "Someone die? Why's the county dead guy here."

"Probably to see me."

"Oh, so that's why he's lurking," she said.

I put the car in park. "What are you talking about?"

"You're having an affair."

"No, I'm not."

"Too bad." She reached for the back door. "Why is this not opening?'

"Child locks."

"Your child is fifteen."

"Habit." I stepped out of the car, opening the back door for my mother.

"Thank God." She too stepped out.

Cody approached us both. "Hey, Al ... Mrs. Hickman."

"My goodness, Cody you grew up."

"I'm almost forty." He leaned down and gave her a quick hug and kiss to the cheek. "You smell really nice."

"Blame her." My mother pointed as she walked to the house. "She doused me with dryer sheets for some reason."

"Go on in, Mom, I'll be right there."

With a "Yeah, yeah" she kept on walking to my door.

"Dryer sheets?" Cody asked.

"I didn't know what else to do to stop the static."

"Well, that's not bad. Hey, um …" He placed his hands in the front pickets of his pants. "You said at the station you would help me."

"I will."

"Good. You have a few minutes, join me for a coffee to talk?"

"Sure, what's going on?"

"I talked to the ME in Jefferson. They had nine people today ignite."

"Oh my God."

"And each day, each prolonged exposure to all this electricity, it's gonna get worse. We need to make sure it doesn't," he said. "So we have to come up with a plan. Something we can do on our own because we aren't going to get permission for it."

"You want to figure out how to turn it all off."

Cody nodded nervously before clearing his throat and saying, "Exactly."

"Alright," I said. "I'm in."

TWELVE
THWARTED OVER COFFEE

"You were in the basement, correct?" Cody asked.

"I was. In the laundry room. No windows, just the vent for the dryer hose."

"Good. Good. No burns?"

I shook my head. "None on me or Sofie."

"What about your mom?"

"She wasn't outside. She has a burn on her hand, she said she got it on the air fryer."

"Here's what I know," Cody said. "If you missed the event, weren't near the sun for the three minutes, you're fine. You weren't compromised. People that weren't outside are showing burns, but it's the ones that were in the sun, in the flash, that are going first."

I lowered my head and lifted my coffee. "Can we stop it?"

"Yeah, we can protect those people, give them time to regenerate, but they cannot have anything around that stimulates the process, at all."

"A camping trip, maybe?"

"You're worried about Gordan," he said.

"I am. Yesterday it was one burn. Now it's a bunch."

"You can't put him in car, Al, you can't. It can be bad. My ME friend in Jefferson said it happened to two people in cars and they crashed killing others. You have to keep him out of the car."

"Well, he walks to work, so that's good."

"This is all going to happen fast. My guess is about three or four days there will be no denying it."

"Do you know of any others like us?" I asked.

"The chief, and a couple people in town. We need to focus on this town. Saving this town." He reached into his pocket and pulled out a folded paper. He undid the fold exposing a map of town. There were X's on the map."

"What are the marks?" I pointed.

"Transformers," he said. "Cell towers. My buddy Pete was not exposed. He works in construction and can get us what we need."

"Can't you just make like an EMP? Doesn't that work?"

Cody smiled. "That's not that easy."

"You want to take them out. Blow them up?"

"Yes."

An, "Uh … not really a good idea," came from behind me. The chief stood there. "Please, Cody and Al, tell me you aren't planning a terror attack on our grid."

"Chief, this is a private conversation," I said. "You don't know what we're talking about."

"Blowing the transformers and cell towers," the chief replied. "I heard you."

"Then you're taking it out of context," I replied.

"Um, I doubt that." He pointed to the map. "Put it away. Put the crazy idea out of your head."

"Chief," Cody said. "Do you not see what is happening?"

"Yeah, I do. I see the alien thing all over again."

"How am I the only one who didn't know about you and the aliens?" I asked.

Chief Harmen pointed at Cody. "I followed you then. I listened, Cody, I can't do the same thing."

"Chief you have bodies."

"Two." The chief held up his fingers. "Two. One an accident and one a murder."

"On the same street."

"Cody. Please. I'm asking you nicely," the chief said. "What I heard you say, I can arrest you. I don't want to do that."

Cody pulled the map forward. "Because I'm your only ME and you'll have more bodies. I'm trying to save this town."

"I'll make you a deal. If I see more proof of this theory, I will help you myself. But we won't blow it up. Deal?"

"Deal," Cody said sulking.

"Have a good evening." The chief walked away.

I leaned over the table. "Are we gonna listen to him?"

"For now. But I'll get the proof. I'll get things ready so when it's time, if we need to, we'll take care of it."

I nodded and sipped my coffee. There was worry on Cody's face and I understood that. He said things were going to get worse and fast.

He was in a stalemate. He wanted badly to save the town, but couldn't.

Not yet.

I knew my husband and mother were in danger. And until we took care of the town, I knew what I had to do to take care of my family.

THIRTEEN

THE SWITCH

I stood in the doorway of the bathroom long before Gordan even knew I was there.

He slathered cream on his burned arms. A white cream that he gingerly tried to smooth over the burns that made it past his elbow.

Finally, he looked up and saw me.

"They're reproducing," I said

"They're just coming out. Don't start."

"Dinner is on the table."

"I'll be right down."

It was hard to believe that something so simple as Cody's theory could cause such tension between us.

I walked down to the dining room, where the grilled chicken, corn, and potatoes sat in the middle of the four candles.

"He'll be right down," I said.

Sofie placed down her phone. "I still don't have a signal."

"Maybe your parents didn't pay the bill," my mother said. "Did you pay the bill, Al?"

"I paid the bill. She doesn't have a signal."

"Strange." Sofie set down her phone. "Oh, well."

My mother reached over and tapped her hand. "That's a very good attitude."

Sofie adored my mother and that was a good thing, because if she didn't, I was certain my mother would have driven her absolutely nuts.

When I told my mother what Sofie had witnessed, my mother went into some sort of weird mode with her.

Of course, it didn't help that Sofie kept saying, "I killed him, Gram, I killed him."

To which my mother replied, "Well, you were trying to help. So don't worry about it."

We sat there waiting, plates empty, until Gordan came down.

I could smell the salve the moment he stepped in.

"Sorry," he said.

"What's going on with your arms?" my mother asked. "Have you seen a doctor?"

"I'm fine." Gordan sat. "Just got injured when I was with George."

"Very scary," my mother said. "You know. George burns. Jan burns. Makes you wonder if something is going on in this neighborhood."

Gordan glanced at me.

"Let's eat." I handed the platter to Gordan.

"What's up with the candles?" Gordan asked.

"Maybe she has an obsession with fire," my mother said.

"Gram." Sofie giggled.

"Did you cook on the grill?" Gordan asked me. "You hate cooking on the grill."

"Well, I think it's a nice change of pace," I replied.

Gordan fixed his plate and looked over when Sofie stood. "Where are you going?"

"To get a drink."

"Can you grab the milk?" he asked.

"Sure. Anyone else need anything?" Sofie asked.

I shook my head, and so did my mother.

She went into the kitchen and returned with a soda for herself and a glass of milk for Gordan. She set it in front of him.

"Thank you, sweetie," he said and lifted it. He made a cringing face after his sip. "Why is the milk warm?"

Sofie answered, "Because the fridge is off."

"The fridge is off?" he asked. "Al, is it broke?"

"No."

"If it's not broke, why is it off?" he questioned.

"It's just off."

Sofie spoke nonchalantly. "I think we have a power outage."

"Yeah, I called the company," I said. "Power is just out."

"Probably why I don't have a phone signal," Sofie said.

"The power has nothing to do with your signal." Gordan lifted his phone. "I don't have one either."

I continued eating, not looking up. But I felt it. I felt him staring at me.

"Al?" Gordan questioned. "Did you shut off the power?'

"What?" I laughed. "Why would I do that?"

"Because of Cody's theory."

My mother asked, "What's Cody's theory?"

"Cody, our resident medical examiner nut job seems to think the sun went haywire," Gordan explained. "Set off some sort of internal turmoil, which is making people suddenly burst into flames when they are near static."

My mother looked at me. "Is that why you had me wear dryer sheets?"

I nodded. "Yes."

"Oh my God," Sofie exclaimed. "Is that what happened to George? He was holding his phone."

"Yes," I replied.

"No," Gordan snapped. "No, it's insane. Do you hear yourself, Al? The sun didn't set off some chain reaction in our bodies. My burns are not from the sun or that flash that happened."

My mother shrugged. "Maybe it's radiation burns."

"That." Gordan pointed at her. "Is far more feasible than the sun causing us to catch fire. Did you shut off the power, Al?"

"Gordan, listen."

"Did you?"

"Yes."

"Al, it's insane. Stop this. Okay. Stop. None of this is happening." He stood up.

"Where are you going? Your dinner will get cold."

"I want my milk cold," he replied. "I'm going to the breaker box."

"You can't." I jumped up. "It's too much current. You're in danger.'

"And you aren't."

"No, me and Sofie were in the basement doing laundry when it happened."

"It's ridiculous, Al." He walked from the room.

I followed. "Okay, let me do it."

"I have it." He walked down the basement steps.

"Gordan, please. Let me put it back on."

"Al, honestly, I have it." He walked to the breaker box.

"Gordan ..."

He opened the cover.

When he did I let out this loud, shrill scream.

He paused. "What is wrong with you?" He looked inside the box. "You turned off the mains." He reached.

I was utterly terrified at that moment, scared for my husband. I was beyond rational.

"Please, don't do it. Please. I'll do it, just ..."

"Stop." He flipped the switch. The lights came on. "See? I'm fine."

I froze and then exhaled. I was overreacting. My fear was for naught.

"Gordan, I'm sorry."

"No, it's fine. Now can we go eat that chicken, it looks…." His eyes drifted from me, getting this deadpan look.

"Gord?"

Suddenly, those same deadpan eyes widened. His hand shot to his chest. "Al, I …"

I watched it happened

His hand lay flush on his chest and from beneath it, his chest was nearly translucent as a blue bright light swirled for a split second.

"Al …" He reached out.

As he did, I watched as his entire being ignited. It started from the inside. I saw it swirling in his chest, illuminating his skin and bones like an orange X-ray. It took only seconds before Gordan's entire torso was engulfed in flames.

It happened so fast, I could barely scream.

I did. I cried for my mom, Sofie, anyone … help.

It was too late.

It was as if Gordan had been hit with some sort of super powerful laser blast or nuclear weapon. Instantly, with his eyes still locked on mine, he incinerated. Like an implosion of his body, it just … bam … gone.

His left arm dropped to the ground landing on the pile of ashes and burned bits of bones.

I couldn't stop screaming.

FOURTEEN
REALITY

If I didn't lose my mind by the end of it all, then I would be lucky.

When Sofie made it down the stairs she just started screaming as well. "Daddy. Daddy."

My mother was calm. Perhaps all the things she saw in her life built up some wall. She stared, a slight look of horror on her face and said, "You were right, Al. Weren't you?"

There was no smoldering like with Jan, probably because he landed on the concrete and not a bed. It took a while for anyone to come.

In fact, my mother said when she called 911 she was put on hold.

Then came the wait.

At first, we waited. We sat on the basement stairs. After twenty minutes and another call to 911, I covered what remained of my husband with a sheet.

After an hour of waiting, we moved upstairs and waited. Sitting on the porch, listening to the sirens that blared in the distance.

We all cried, it seemed surreal. Our dinner was still on the table. Gordan's plate was still perfectly made and untouched.

I couldn't believe what was happening. Far too much in shock to really register the events of the night, I sat in a state of disbelief, gripping my daughter's hand, hoping it all was a nightmare I'd wake up from soon.

There were no sirens when they arrived at our home. They came without fanfare.

Three vehicles pulled up.

A squad car, the county coroner SUV, and the van from Weston Funeral Home.

All three parked in front of my home.

The chief along with Jenkins stepped out at the same time as Cody. The three of them walked toward us on the porch while two men from Weston hung back.

Cody placed his hand on my shoulder as he walked in. "I'm sorry."

I nodded.

"Where is he?"

"In the basement."

His hand slid off and I stared at the chief.

"Al," he said. "I am very, very sorry. You want to tell me what happened?"

"I tried. I tried to stop it from happening."

"What do you mean?" he asked.

"I saw it growing on him. His arms. It was one burn last night, then by the time he came home, both his arms were just covered. So I shut off all the power. Everything. Just like Cody said."

The chief looked by me to the house. "Your lights are on now."

"That's why."

"Al, I'm confused."

"I shut off the power, he got mad and put the breaker back on," I said. "A few seconds later he just ... I saw ..." I gazed up at him. "His whole chest lit up from within. For a split second I saw his beating heart."

"You don't think anything with the breaker box could have caused this?"

I shook my head. "No, this was an inner explosion. He felt it, he looked at me and knew what was happening. He didn't scream like George though. He just ..." I closed my eyes.

"Do you think ...?"

"Chief," Jenkins interrupted him. "There is no other explanation. Not for Gordan, not for the others."

The chief nodded sadly. "No. You're right."

"By others you mean Jan and George?" I asked.

Jenkins shook his head. "We have been on calls on night. About the third on, we just called Weston to come along."

"How many?" I questioned.

I heard my screen door open behind me and Cody answered. "Nine not including Gordan and he won't be the last." He stepped off the porch and signaled to the Weston men.

85

"Same?" the chief asked.

"Same," Cody answered.

"Ma'am," one of the Weston men said as he passed. "We are very sorry."

"Thank you." I closed my eyes tighter, trying not to see the body bag they carried.

The chief informed me of what was going to happen. "Al, Weston will take Gordan. Clean up everything in the basement. Tomorrow they will be cremating the rest of the remains. They will contact you. I'm sorry, this is the way it has to be."

"Do you believe me now?" Cody asked hard. "Seriously. Do you believe me?"

"Cody I never said I didn't," the chief said. "I just said the plan was too much when the news hadn't said anything. Besides, she shut off the lights. Gordan ignited anyhow."

"Because," I replied, "he put them back on. He was close, too close."

"She's right," Cody said. "Once they are at that point they can not be exposed to any power, any large noise, vibration or static. Nothing. The body has to regenerate. Be proactive, Chief. Take measures now before the news is announced and people go nuts."

"You're right," the chief said. "So let's come up with a plan. A viable plan that doesn't involve terrorist activity." He tilted his head toward the radio on his collar and spoke. "This is Chief Harmen."

I watched as he listened with a saddened look.

"Copy. We're on our way."

Jenkins asked, "Another?"

"Four," the chief replied. "Gas and Go. One ignition took out the whole place."

"Jesus," Jenkins gasped.

"Fire department is in route. Cody? Meet you there?" the chief asked.

"Yeah, I'll inform Weston."

The chief and Jenkins arrived in a whimper and left in a bang. Their sirens blasted as they peeled out.

All over the town, I could hear the sirens.

It was going to be a long, sleepless, heartbreaking night for a lot of people and not just my family.

FIFTEEN
IN DEEP

I barely slept. In fact, none of us did.

We stayed in the living room. I curled up on the recliner, while Sofie cuddled with my mother on the couch. I hated that I was frightened about that. What if my mother ignited? I checked her. The only burn that she had was on her hand and it was healing. No other burns at all. Maybe my mother had been spared exposure. After all, she believed that when you closed the blinds and drapes during the day it kept the house cool.

It was unseasonably warm and knowing my mother she didn't want the AC on any earlier than she needed to put it on.

During the night, for my mother's sake, I powered the house down again. I kept the windows open for a breeze. The temperature dropped enough to make it tolerable.

In the morning, I made eggs on the grill along with percolator coffee. But we definitely woke to a different world.

I expected the funeral home to call so I turned on my phone, staying outside with it, certain Weston's would call early.

I had my coffee out there.

I knew ... knew things were different. Something had changed in the six or seven hours since I closed the front door for the night.

It was quiet, no more sirens, not much street or people noise at all. A few trails of smoke remained in the sky.

There was still an internet connection and I went online.

Surely, the world had fallen apart, and it would be all over the news.

Nothing.

I scrolled, checked, and searched and the only thing close to it was the story of a local anchorman in Phoenix that was electrocuted on the air.

A part of me started to wonder if it was just our area, our town, or even state.

It didn't matter because my world and everything that mattered was there in the town with me.

While I was fairly confident Sofie and I were safe, I'd already lost my husband and I wasn't about to lose my mother.

Plans had to be made, even on my part, to do everything I could to protect her.

After giving my mother and Sofie their breakfast, I decided to go to the store. Maybe walk to Weston's first, see what was happening.

Moving about town would allow me to gauge how things were.

It was quiet. Last I heard there were fifteen thousand men, women, and children in our town. I wondered how many were tucked safely inside and below when the flash happened.

Thinking of the children in town simply broke my heart. How many of them would suffer? How many parents would have to witness a horrendous fate to their child?

I took the long way to Weston's, walking through the neighborhood instead of down the main street. I needed to get a feel for things, and it was hard to judge. Was it just a normal Wednesday and everyone was working? Maybe it didn't feel that way because I knew things weren't normal. I saw only two cars driving and one person sitting on their porch.

A whole different perspective hit me when I turned the corner and saw Weston Funeral Home.

There was a line that extended out the main front doors, across the porch and down the driveway.

A line of people.

Voices churned together like the humming of a swarm of bees. It was so steady; it had a vibration to it. I tried to see what was going on. Was there a funeral service for someone really popular and everyone was waiting in line to get in?

There had to be a hundred people in line, that had to be it.

I wasn't there to pay my respects, I was only there for Gordan. So bypassing the line, I walked straight to the front doors.

A gentleman in a suit stood out front and I heard him say to a woman, "Ma'am we have been here all night. We're all tired. We're trying to be respectful of everyone's grief."

"Hey!" Someone grabbed for my arm. "Hey." It wasn't a pleasant 'hey' either. The grip was strong and the woman pulled at me.

"Excuse me." I reached to remove her hand, when I did, my eyes froze and locked on the burns on her arm.

"Where are you going? Get in the back of the line."

"I'm not here for the funeral. I'm here because they picked up my husband last night and I just need to know what's going on."

"Then get in line," she said. "We're all here for the same reason."

"Everyone?" I asked in shock.

"Everyone."

I slipped back from her turning my head slowly and looking at the people once more.

All those people.

I was mortified.

Stepping away from the crowd, I pulled out my phone to text Cody.

Cody, whose number two days earlier, I never had, or thought I would have, was the number one person I was texting.

I'm at Weston's. So many people here, I wrote.

We lost a lot of people last night. It's not stopped, he replied.

91

Briefly I closed my eyes and whispered out a "Jesus," before replying again. *Did you meet with the chief?*

We're meeting at two. He's gathering people that weren't exposed. If you feel up to stopping by, please do.

I might. Thanks. Before ending the conversation, I wished him luck, then put my phone away.

I wasn't going to wait in line. I'd come back, nothing was going to change if I waited or went, the end result was all the same. My husband was gone.

All that remained of him were ashes.

Cody's plan to go dark ran through my mind as I made my way back home, this time through town.

Everyone relied on technology. Lights, phones, internet. Even I had a hard time putting my phone away. I wasn't certain that people would relinquish it with ease. Many would fight and say it was bull. They'd want more proof. It was the nature of the human race to question. It certainly was the motto of our 'show me' state.

Then again, watching someone erupt into flames should be proof enough.

As I passed Green Leaf Grocery, I started thinking about food and ways to prepare meals on the grill or maybe not even cook at all. It was warm.

Cucumber salad and sandwiches sounded like a good meal on a hot day, so I went inside.

I picked up one of those little baskets, draping the handle over my forearm. I looked at everyone I walked by, my eyes immediately spotting burns. Some worse than others.

In the deli, I stayed clear of people, just in case.

It was busier than I expected it to be.

People were talking about what was happening.

"I heard Rob Stewart died last night."

"It's radiation, I tell you. Radiation. Look at my arm."

It went on and on.

"Seventy-four," the deli clerk called out.

That was me. I held up my paper ticket and stepped to the counter. After dropping the ticket in the container, I smiled at the older gentleman next to me then placed my order.

Every second was nerve wracking. I didn't want to be around people. Every electrical device seemed to be loud to me. The phones dinging, the air conditioner humming.

The older gentleman next to me reached for his pack of deli meat a few seconds before I grabbed my final one. He placed it in his cart, paused and hunched.

I expected flames. *Oh, no,* I thought, *I do not want to see this again.*

Before I could make a quick escape, he just tumbled. Tilted to the right and fell to the floor.

There were a few voices that erupted in shock and screams.

"Stay back," a woman shouted. "I'm a nurse." She rushed to the man, shoving his buggy out of the way and dropping to the floor next to him. "Someone call 911, please." She felt for a pulse, then listened for a breath. "Is there an AED?"

At first it didn't register what she was asking for, then it hit me.

AED.

Automated External Defibrillator.

Electrical current.

I stuttered out, "No," but she didn't hear me.

The deli man brought her the case, and she immediately began to open it. It was clear she was trained and knew exactly what she was doing.

"No," the words blurted out. "No, you can't."

"I'm a professional. I know what I'm doing," she said. "Please. Everyone back up."

She turned on the device and ripped open his shirt, moving quickly.

"Press pad firmly to patient's skin," said the computerized voice from the AED.

She wiped off his skin with gauze, opened the pads, peeled back the sticky parts and put them on his chest.

"Analyzing heart rhythm," the computer instructed. *"Do not touch patient."*

"Stay clear," the nurse said.

"Preparing shock," recited the device. *"Move away from the patient."* A pause. *"Press red flashing button to deliver shock."*

Watching her finger move to the red heart shaped button happened in slow motion. I tried to back up, but people crowded, blocking me in.

I held my breath.

I waited.

Nothing.

"Shock delivered. It is now safe to touch the patient. Start CPR."

My exhale was heavy. I fully expected with that shock for there to be some sort of ignition. There wasn't.

Not then. Not from the AED.

She cupped her hands, placing them on his chest and on the fourth compression, her hands sunk straight through his torso. Her depression was like a thumb against the spark wheel on a disposable lighter.

Flash.

A huge blast of fire erupted from his chest, immediately engulfing the nurse.

She screamed so loud, so shrill, but they were nearly buried by the screams of everyone around that witnessed it.

I was certain people were rushing to help. I saw them run her way.

Me ... right thing to do or wrong.

I ran.

I couldn't help it.

Grocery basket still dangling from my arm, I ran and kept on running until I was out of that store and halfway down the block.

SIXTEEN
SEVEN BLOCKS OF HELL

My house wasn't far at all from the small grocery store in our town.

Four blocks and at the police station take another right. Three more blocks was our house.

A short distance, but it was seven blocks through the end of the world.

At first I was in denial.

It wasn't real. It wasn't real.

I was stuck in a time loop or a bad dream, both of those were more believable than someone just bursting into flames.

After running from the store, I waited. Waited for people to run out, for the police to come or fire department.

Holding that basket like Little Red Riding Hood, I turned facing the direction of the store, watching …

I felt guilty for running, of being scared of what I witnessed and not doing anything to help.

Within seconds people ran out of the store screaming as if there were some sort of active shooter.

Yet, no sirens ever came.

Then I watched a woman run out, her phone was to her ear, possibly calling for help and she, as if blasted by an extra-terrestrial laser, exploded and crumbled into ashes on the sidewalk.

My mind screamed, "oh my God," over and over and I spun around again to run.

At that point the police station or home was the destination I had in mind.

But not a few feet into the second block, I was trapped inside *War of the Worlds* when two more running people from the store just disintegrated.

Then it all just erupted.

It no longer was George, Jenny, or my husband, it was random people, left and right. Igniting into flames and collapsing to the ground. One by one. No rhyme or reason. Unsuspecting innocent people who didn't see their fate coming.

They didn't even have time to scream.

I kept running, each step I heard this high pitch sound, squealing like a cat. Short and loud.

I heard the blaring siren and watched the squad car zoom by me. Just as it did, with a quick shift of my eyes, I saw another car. It barreled down the street, hit a truck, kept its course and careened my way. Flames shot from both the driver and passenger window, the windshield was blackened, and the car jumped the sidewalk.

I dove out of the way a split second before it crashed into the store front window of Babette's Treasures.

My entire being shook. It missed me. It just … missed me.

Without looking back, I left. The sound returned.

Squeal. Squeal.

I was running through some sort of video game where there was no escape, no next level of relief.

With unsteady and rubbery legs, I ran forward. At that point I watched every step I took, looking around making sure another car didn't come in my direction.

The squeal noise was steady, so close. Continuous.

What was it?

I've always watched those scenes in movies. Panic on the streets, people racing in no particular directions, crying out and screaming.

That was our town.

It had been transformed into something I didn't recognize, and it seemed the more upset the people were, the faster they ran and cried out, the faster they were no more.

I went from walking from my house in a state of despair to running for my home frightened out of my mind.

"Al, Al," my name was called.

I had made it to the police station.

Cody stood out front by his car. "Al, what are you seeing? What's going on?" He grabbed for me.

Was he seriously asking me that question?

Didn't he know? Didn't he see?

Slowly his head turned and his eyes widened. "Oh my God."

Did he hear it? Did he also hear that squeal sound?

I couldn't even speak. I couldn't be rational enough to form words. I pushed him away, and with a turn of my body, that grocery basket hit into him as I ran for my street.

The chaos of the main street was behind me and the quiet of our road was welcoming.

I didn't know if I was out of breath from running or was having a heart attack. My chest was heavy.

Without the sirens, the screams of chaos, that noise that followed me suddenly wasn't a mystery.

When I slowed down I realized it was me.

My own panic sounds, wheezing out an emotional breath with every step I ran. I didn't even recognize my own produced sounds of horror.

My pace went from running, down to a brisk pace, to a walk.

A block from my home I knew I had made it.

The echoes of madness flowed my way from the town square but it wasn't loud.

Some of my neighbors slowly came from their houses, curious as to what was going on.

I wanted to tell them go back inside, shut off the power and hide.

How insane would I sound?

Even though my rationale told me I wasn't in danger, a part of me didn't want to take a chance.

I just wanted to get my mother and daughter and find a quiet place without power or static or anything that could cause one of us to ignite.

I just didn't understand how it all happened the way it did.

George burned slow.

Jenny did as well or at least it looked it.

I watched it happen to Gordan.

Yet, the people on the street running just exploded. It was instantaneous. Was it because the transformation internally made it happen faster or did external factors play a role into the way and speed it went down?

"Al…"

The call of my name sounded weak and desperate.

Standing in front of my own driveway, ready to go into the safety of my home, Bill staggered to me.

He staggered like a drunk, moving left and right, unable to walk a straight line.

"Al …" He extended his arm as he walked to me.

When I saw him I knew instantly.

Seeing Bill gave me answers I didn't register at that moment, but I would.

What happened around people, what people were exposed to determined how it happened within them.

Unlike the people running and screaming. Unlike those on their phones, touching electric or exposed to loud noises, Bill literally was a slow burn.

What was once only his arms covered with blisters and burns was now his entire body, head to toe. Every single square inch of his body was blackened. His skin bubbled. A volatile furnace burned within his body, a fire coursed through his veins instead of blood. The fire that formed beneath his skin glowed like lava in the fissure vents of a volcano.

"Tell my kids …" Bill reached for me. "I love them."

"Bill," I wept as I said his name.

"Help … me … Al."

His charred fingers grazed my left arm and I instinctively stepped back.

Why?

Why did I do that?

The moment he touched me, his hand dropped to the ground before his body turned smoldering red and nothing was left to keep him standing.

As Bill's body became nothing more than a pile of embers, I did nothing.

There was zero left inside of me.

I couldn't scream, I couldn't cry. I could only stand there and watch him burn.

That second became the moment everything changed within me.

SEVENTEEN
AFTERMATH BEGINNING

In the span of ten minutes on a spring morning, it simply became too much.

There were too many bodies to collect. It happened so fast, so many people died, there was no means to tell who was who.

Ashes to Ashes.

Piles of remains scattered about the street. Ashes that would disappear should a single rain shower happen.

For dust you are and to dust you will return.

All I could do after Bill died in front of me was walk up the path and into my home.

I stood with the front door behind me in a state of shock.

"Mommy, I saw." Sofie raced to me. "I saw what happened to Bill."

Unable to speak, I just turned my head and looked at her with wide eyes.

"Are you okay?" she asked.

"Al," my mother walked up to me. "Why are you holding the grocery basket? Did you steal those?"

When I was young, a teenager, same age as Sofie, I watched a movie called, *Body Snatchers*. In it the people had been carbon copied but they weren't themselves. It happened when they slept. Those who wanted to hold on to their humanity didn't fall asleep. I remember a scene in the movie when the lead actor walked up to someone she thought was unchanged, still human. But he wasn't. He suddenly widened his mouth, pointed and made this sound.

A scream of sorts but more of a calling card to alert the others of a 'human.'

I felt like that scene in the movie.

I felt like the alien inhabited body.

"Al, did you steal that?" my mother asked.

A slow turn of my head to her and I just broke, lost it. My jaw dropped and I groaned out long and high pitched. Like some sort of mental break down.

I just know that I no longer saw my mother, I was mentally transported outside of my home and everyone, all around me was burning.

I was in a nightmare and the next thing I knew I was in my bed, opening my eyes and seeing Cody.

In fact, when I saw him I was convinced I had woken from a nightmare. That for some reason nothing really had happened. That I missed our coffee meeting by sleeping in.

That was my rationale for Cody being in my bedroom.

That lasted only a minute.

Then I realized, I must have passed out. Everything really did happen.

"Is she okay?" Sofie asked.

I looked to my right, Sofie and my mother stood there.

"Al," Cody called my name. "Can you talk? Say something."

It took a few seconds and I spoke, "They're all dead, aren't they?"

Cody didn't answer my question, he stared at me for a few seconds, then took the stethoscope from around his neck and placed it in his medical bag.

He stood. "She'll be fine. She isn't in a catatonic state, which is what I worried about."

"What?" I asked.

"I'll explain. What's the last thing you remember?"

"Coming in the house," I replied.

"Okay. Maureen," he spoke to my mother. "Bring her back downstairs, we'll all talk." He turned and walked out of the room.

"Let me help," my mother reached for me.

"Mom, I got it. Thanks." I swung my legs over the bed and that was when I noticed the window. The lighting was different. When I went to the store the sun was bright, now it was dim, a weird overcast. "Did something happen again with the sun?" I asked.

Sofie shook her head. "No. Why?"

"It seems like the sun is hiding."

"That's because it's evening," my mother replied.

"Evening?" I asked.

Sofie nodded. "Seven."

"Seven!" I spoke in shock. "It can't be seven, I was just in the living room. It was ten when I left."

"Yeah," Sofie said. "It was. You've been out of it that long."

<><><><>

I quickly learned what transpired.

My mother and Sofie both told me.

When I walked in, something I remembered doing, I didn't speak. My mother said I had this strange look and my skin was pasty white.

Then I started making some strange noise.

All of that, I sort of remembered.

However, I didn't recall dropping the shopping basket, racing upstairs and after another five minutes of solid screaming, I lay on the bed, on top of the covers and stared.

That was how Cody found me.

Lying flat on my back, staring out. Not speaking.

None of which I remember.

No one called Cody, he happened to stop by.

Not to say my mother and Sofie didn't call for help. They did. But no one came.

"I think," Cody said, sitting at my dining room table. "You shut down. You emotionally and mentally shut down. You're lucky you snapped out of it. There was a chance you wouldn't."

"Cody, so much happened today."

"And you mentally retreated through most of it," he said.

"What? How? The store …"

"Al, it's just all come to a head. It's only going to get worse," Cody explained.

"Did the news break? Did …"

"It doesn't matter what the news said or did," Cody said. "Maureen, show her your arm."

My heart skipped a beat and then started thumping out of control. My mom extended her arm. On her wrist was a burn.

"This is happening. This is real. We can't worry about the rest of the world, we need to worry about here," Cody said. "So few of us were below. So few of us weren't affected. So the few of us spared need to make sure we protect those who are vulnerable."

"So many died," I said.

"Yeah, and I want to stop more from dying," Cody replied. "We can. Now, it takes seven years for the entire body to replace every single cell. But cells replace every day. In order for someone to get out of the danger zone, those affected cells need to regenerate. It can take weeks, months or years. But until then, we need to make sure nothing causes it to get worse. We need to let them heal."

My mother asked, "How?"

Sofie replied. "Turning off the lights, right? No power. No energy."

"No nothing," Cody added. "Nothing. Everything needs to be eliminated."

"I don't understand," I said. "What do you mean?"

"Everything and anything can and will set it off. Electronics, vibrations, noise, excitement."

Cody must have noticed the confusion on my face. He stared at me for a second.

"How?" Sofie asked. "How can excitement cause anything?"

He explained. "In the upper quadrant of the heart, the atria, it produces an electrical stimulus every sixty to a hundred beats. Under normal circumstances. The faster the heart beats, the more electrical stimulus. The more that happens, the more spark to the cells." He looked around. "Your mom is a relatively calm person, your little episode jump started her heart."

"Her arm," I said.

Cody nodded. "That is why we all need to shut down. Just shut down. Lights, cars, emotions, everything. Everything until people start to heal."

I asked, "Is that possible?"

"We'll have to make it possible."

"Jesus Christ," my mother blurted out. "How do you expect that to be possible? There's no way."

"There is," Cody replied. "We'll have to be disciplined, and we will be, even if we have to enforce it to save lives, we will, and we'll have to live in a dark … quiet world."

Still in a semi state of shock, I listened trying to absorb all that Cody was saying.

Some made sense. Some didn't.

I knew one thing, everything was about to change.

And it scared the hell out of me.

SELFISH

EIGHTEEN
SPECIAL DELIVERY

Day Four

It was an unbelievably long night. I went back and forth between tired and scared, crying and angry. Barely sleeping and when I did, I woke up just as fast as I fell asleep.

Spurts of rest.

I guessed that would change once I was emotionally grounded.

For the time being, I felt broken and confused. My heart ached so bad for Gordan and I felt guilty as well because the events occurring seemed to keep popping into my mind, pushing his death to the back for a few moments.

I couldn't help it.

Cody's visit the night before told us about the only way those affected could survive.

Silence.

Yet, screaming in the distance, every five minutes, all night long were sirens.

Our town had erupted.

Silence was the last thing happening.

Cody likened what was happening inside people to a low heat under a pot of sauce on the stove.

The boiling point of the pot on the stove was the ignition point in the human bodies hit by the flash.

Keep it at the same heat, eventually it would boil. Increase the heat, it would come to a boil faster. Turn off the heat, it would cool.

In a cooking analogy, we needed the bodies to cool.

Turn off the heat.

Every sound, vibration, electronic device, raised the proverbial heat.

But how would they go about doing it? How would they get people to not only voluntarily live in the dark but to live without every other modern convenience, all while staying quiet?

It wasn't going to happen.

Not easily.

I couldn't even stay away from my phone long enough and I wasn't in danger. At least I didn't think so. I went into the yard, as far away as I could from the house to see if I could find out anything on the news.

Nothing.

It was then I realized that a lot of the articles hadn't been updated since the 'so-called' terror attacks.

Unlike any other times that attacks happened, there were no follow up stories. No president making vows to find those responsible. It was as if it happened and the truth was far worse. How does one report that anyone who'd been exposed could instantaneously ignite?

Would people even believe it?

I wanted badly to turn on the television. To see what was being said. I feared that though because my mother needed to be sheltered and calm, whether she wanted to or not.

Perhaps because I placed myself in the dark, I was unaware of whatever breaking news was being reported.

There were so many questions I needed answers to.

How far spread was it? Were people lining up in the ER over suspicious burns?

If any electronic, vibration, noise or excitement caused the internal spark, how would they get the news out without using noise or electronics to make people aware?

The reasonable way was word of mouth. In our town, it was small enough that it was completely possible.

The bigger cities ... it was inconceivable. A part of me believed that the larger places would just let things run its course.

I powered down my phone not wanting to chance it ringing in the house. After placing it in my pocket I headed to the back porch, when I saw him.

A younger man, maybe in his late twenties. He came from the side of the house and lifted his hand in a wave. He wore dress pants and one of those golf style shirts with an emblem on the chest.

What was he doing? Who was he and why was he in my yard?

Apprehensively, I approached him.

He whispered, "I didn't want to knock or ring the bell. Please tell me I didn't scare you."

He knew.

Just by the way he spoke and how timid he acted, he knew about the events.

"No." I shook my head.

"Good. I worry, you know with things …"

"I'm fine. I wasn't exposed."

"Were you below?" he asked.

"Yes."

"Me, too. I'm trying to be quiet when I go to a house. Hoping to see someone without having to knock. That's why I came around back."

"I understand."

It was then I noticed not only the emblem on his shirt, but he held something in his hand.

The emblem was Weston Funeral Home.

"I'm very sorry for your loss." He handed me a small box. It was no bigger than six inches by six inches.

I glanced down to the box. It was Gordan. The love of my life had been reduced to fitting in a box. That was his finale in life and he deserved so much more.

"You're delivering loved ones?" I asked.

He nodded. "I have to. Again, I'm sorry. It's all we can do. We're going to be working around the clock."

"How many … how many people?"

"So far," he replied. "At least twenty percent of the town."

"That's three thousand people," I said.

"I know. And we haven't even gotten them all. We're trying."

"Good luck."

He nodded again and walked away. He walked strangely as if deliberately trying to tread lightly. As he left my backyard, I followed him. He was delivering loved ones, but how?

Then I saw.

Perched on the sidewalk in front of my house was a red wagon. The kind we used to use when we took Sofie to the zoo. From where I stood, I could see it was filled with stacks of boxes similar to the ones I held.

All those people, lost, and it was that young man's job to deliver them and do so quietly.

I felt horrible for him. What a terrible job to do. He lifted the handle and moved at a snail's pace down the street in his daunting task.

He didn't have to walk far. Two houses and he stopped.

The Graham family.

Twenty percent of the town was lost. Friends, neighbors, people I may have only said hello to. Gone in a flash.

I hoped it was the end, no more would be lost. I knew that wouldn't be the case.

It was far from over. And unless something was done to stop it, I knew, as it added up, as we lost more people, that young man would never be able to deliver the remains, no matter how diligent he was.

NINETEEN
AVON CALLING

My mother was resentful.

"I'm old," she told me. "I don't care."

It's hard to believe that your parents are old. I supposed one day I'd look at my mother and see that she had aged. Until then I insisted she wasn't old and I wasn't ready to give her up.

"Al, I get the lights being off," she said. "I get the no phones or TV. Heck, I am happy to read a book, but damn it, I am not going to lock myself in a room and never move."

"It's not forever, Mom, it's not."

"I realize that. But I can't hide, Al. You're not going to find a lot of people willing to hide. I should be able to walk around."

"You heard Cody, if your heart elevates …"

"Then so be it. I'm not saying I won't follow the rules, I'm just saying I won't go to the extreme. I will walk. I'll go outside and that starts with burying my son-in-law."

Burying Gordan.

Apparently funerals were put on hold and so were cemetery rituals.

I took a shovel and went into the backyard, and I dug a hole.

I never imagined I would be a widow, let alone putting my husband's ashes in the ground in the backyard.

The entire time I dug that hole, I kept seeing my neighbor peek out the window. Standing in the kitchen, leaning out trying to act all inconspicuous.

Several times I made eye contact with her. She and her husband hadn't lived in the house very long, at least I didn't think so, so I didn't really know her well.

Hell, I didn't even know her name.

When I finished the hole, I walked to the edge of the yard and found the biggest stone I could.

When Gordan and I moved into the house, the patio was nothing more than a series of large flat stones. It probably looked amazing when it was first done. But time made the rocks look green and weeds poke through.

Instead of getting rid of the rocks completely, Gordan threw them in the wooded area behind the shed.

I found one of those flat rocks, went into the shed and grabbed a small can of paint.

I wrote his name on that rock, along with 'loving husband' and year of birth and death.

The rock was heavy and I carried it to the hole.

It would serve as his headstone.

I stood on the freshly dug grave staring at the stone, knowing I would have my own ceremony soon. I lifted my eyes to see the woman next door still staring at me.

Stepping away from the grave, I kept my eyes on her and lifted my arms as if to say, 'What?'

She moved away from the window.

I thought that was that, until I heard her back door open.

She crept to me, it was strange. Did she realize what was happening?

There was a certain fearful look on her face, it was drawn and pale. She wasn't an old woman, young, maybe in her twenties with thick brown hair, yet the look on her face aged her.

She pursed her lips, moistened them and spoke softly. "Did you lose a pet?"

I was confused by that, then I realized the hole I dug wasn't that big. "No," I replied. "My husband."

"I'm sorry."

'Thank you. If you don't mind, we're going to bury him."

I glanced over, looking at my house, knowing my daughter and mother were inside waiting on me.

"Okay," she said nodding nervously. "I'll let you go." She stepped back and tilted her head, her eyes stared at my arms. "You don't have the marks."

"Excuse me?" I asked.

"The marks from the flare," she replied. "You don't have them."

I shook my head. "No, I wasn't exposed."

"Good. That's good." She stepped back. "Again, I'm sorry about your husband."

"Wait … did you watch the news? Are they announcing that the flash is causing things to happen? Is that how you knew?" I asked, because I knew I hadn't read anything and the chief and Cody hadn't put the word out.

She shook her head. "My brother told me about it four days before it happened. He runs this solar watch website. He predicted the event. Just not what it would do. He said to stay below. I did. I locked myself in the cold cellar. If you don't know … turn off all power, don't use the phone. He thinks it's causing people's internal organs to melt. Doesn't make sense."

"No, it doesn't. But it's true, in a way. That's what …" I glanced down to the hole. "That's what happened to Gordan. So you and your husband were safe?"

She shook her head. "I was the only one below. My husband went into Kansas City. He had a meeting the next day. I haven't heard from him."

"Maybe you will. But, I don't want to be rude, I just …"

She drew up an apologetic look and walked back toward her house, just as she walked inside, the chief came into my backyard.

Up went my hands again, and instead of tremendous sadness, I felt annoyed.

Really. I just wanted to bury my husband. I had to pull myself together. How would he know? He didn't mean to interrupt.

"Sorry to bother you, Al," the chief spoke softly. "Just…"
He handed me a sheet of paper. "I need your help. Just when you get a chance …"

"I am trying to bury Gordan, Chief."

"I'm sorry. I just … Tonight we're meeting at seven. We need to get the word out and I need the help of all those who weren't exposed to help. Plus, there's other things we have to do. But in order to spare lives, we can only ask those not exposed."

I glanced down to the paper.

"When you get a chance. Give that a read. It's brief. It explains it simply and we are going to go door to door with those."

I nodded. "I'll help."

"Thank you."

"The woman next door … she wasn't exposed."

"Avon Mersing?" he asked.

"I don't know her name. She lives next door."

"Yeah." He nodded. "That's Avon Mersing."

"You say the name like I should know who she is."

"You should but … she's a little … she's not all there, Al."

"Well, not all there or not, we need all the help we can get."

"You're right. I'll go speak to her," the chief said. "See you tonight at seven."

After reiterating a yes, I walked back to my house. I just wanted to clean up, be with my family and bury my husband.

That was all I could think about at that moment.

TWENTY
THE PLAN

Due to recent solar events that have caused internal reactions, effectivey immediately we are asking all residents to power down for thirty days.

That was what the flyer said. Obviously, the chief didn't write it and obviously they weren't being realistic.

No one was going to voluntarily power down.

Unless, like me, they believed what was happening. Nothing in that flyer sounded as if the situation was life threatening.

I would bring it up at the meeting.

Like a thief in the night, I oh-so quietly retrieved Sofie's bike from the garage. Because I didn't want the rolling vibration to affect my mother, I carried it with Sofie's help, up the stairs and outside.

"Can't I go?" Sofie asked. "I was below when the flash happened."

"I know. And I'll make sure they use your help, but I need you to stay with Grandma, okay. I don't trust her.'

"What do you mean?"

"I mean, if we both go, she'll turn on the power and watch TV. I don't want her near the breaker box."

"You have a point."

"I do." I kissed Sofie on the cheek. "I shouldn't be long and I'll let you know everything that is happening."

I walked the bike a half of block, before climbing on and slowly, steadily peddling down the street.

Evening was setting in and I could see how many of the houses still were using power. The sound of the air conditioning hum filled the air, it was almost as if I could hear it more than usual.

While there weren't as many cars on the road, when I hit the main street I saw two drive by.

How was the chief supposed to convince people to give up electricity, phones and cars when the entire street was still lit up?

It was literally a danger zone and no wonder so many deaths happened right there the day before.

I could see it in my mind, reliving every scream, crash and burn.

When the lights go out, there is a certain quiet that comes with it.

That wasn't happening in our town.

The neon open light above the door of Schmitty's Bar and Grill flashed and music carried out to the street as I passed it.

People walked in and out.

Not a care in the world.

Twenty percent of their fellow neighbors literally bit the dust and karaoke and Bud Light specials took first priority.

I arrived at the station. Emergency lights were on, but the exterior spotlight or anything electronic wasn't.

"Hey, Al." Jenkins looked up at me from his paperwork as he stood at the front desk.

Immediately, I got sick to my stomach when I saw him.

His arms, neck, parts of his cheek, all burned.

"Hey, Jenkins."

"They're in the back" he said. "The boardroom."

"Thank you."

It registered he told me 'boardroom,' it surprised me that our little precinct would have a boardroom.

I also wasn't sure who 'they' were, I knew the chief and Cody would be there.

I found the room, it was way in the back by the holding cell area. The door was open and in my approach I saw Cody and the chief. When I stepped inside, I saw my neighbor Avon, along with six other people.

One of them was Martin Leon or something like that. He worked at the post office. A little older than me, but he had this 'irritated at the world' attitude about everything. Every time I ran into him he was complaining.

And he was one of the few people in that room.

That was it?

That was the extent of those not affected.

"Come on in, Al, close the door," the chief said. "We've been waiting on you."

"I'm not late," I said.

"I know."

I closed the door and turned back around. "Why is there karaoke two doors down?"

The man in the room named Martin, replied. "It's Thursday, that's why."

I shook my head slightly. "Yeah, but the lights, music ... aren't we promoting no energy and noise?"

The chief nodded. "Yes, but what am I supposed to do, walk in there and shut them down?"

"Yes."

"No, Al, it's not that simple," he replied "We need to convince them individually. That's why we're here. To discuss it and a course of action."

Cody spoke up. "We pass out the flyers, answer any questions and hope that most people listen."

"They won't," Avon said. "They'll look at this"—she lifted the flyer—"and think we're crazy and trust me, I know crazy."

At that second, I noticed everyone in the room nodded in agreement. I made a mental note to find out what the hell it was that I didn't know about Avon, that everyone else did.

"While I don't know what she means about the crazy thing," I said, "I agree. You need to be more specific, give them a place to ask questions, or lie."

"Lie?" The chief asked.

"Lie. Make up something they may find more believable than a solar event. I don't know like ..." I raised my shoulder and fluttered my lips, "alien invasion."

At that second, right after I said it, it was as if I said the most offensive thing.

Everyone gasped.

"Oh, come on," someone said.

"Really, Al?" asked the chief. "Was that necessary?"

"You disappoint me," said Cody.

"Talk about insensitive," Martin commented.

I was baffled. What the hell did I say?

The chief held up his hand. "Let's chalk it up to Al's poor timing and humor. But I see what she means. A lie might be more believable than the truth. But we have to do our best to convince them."

"I will do my best," Cody said, "to answer any questions. We need to keep these people alive. Keep them alive long enough to heal."

"Is there any way to heal them faster?" I asked. "Protect them even more?"

"I don't know," Cody said. "I don't."

"What about testing?" I asked.

"Testing involves invasive procedures that can put them in the danger we are avoiding."

"What about getting people to volunteer?" I asked. "Volunteer to be tested, to maybe find a way."

Another eruption of groans.

"She just doesn't stop," Martin said. "Insensitive to personal trauma, suggesting human guinea pigs. Why don't you volunteer, Al, huh? Why don't you sign right up."

"I would if I wasn't folding laundry when the flash happened," I snapped.

"Okay. Alright." The chief raised his hand. "Admittedly, Cody needs to learn more. He does. We'll work on how to do that. But the point of this meeting isn't to pressure Cody, it's to get people to power down. I know they aren't going to do that with ease. Tomorrow morning, we all go door to door."

Cody added, "There will be questions, try your best to answer."

Martin spoke up, "They'll think, 'oh not me.' Eventually though, I think, when they see those who aren't powering down are … well … vanishing, they'll change their minds. Sooner than later."

"We have another problem," the chief said. "Food. This town has what the Grocer has and that's it. Right now the world news is quiet, they don't know. But as soon as folks figure out things are gonna get bad there is going to be a run for food. And what's in the store and the warehouses are it. At least for a long time."

"It won't be just us," Cody said. "It will be everyone in the area for miles."

"Those not affected," the chief continued, "are at an advantage. We can get around electricity We can drive a car or truck. So before the world goes mad, which is going to happen, I want a team to go to Boehm's Warehouse. Miller has two tractor trailers. They're a quarter mile out of town. Two teams. Raid the warehouse and stash the trucks."

I spoke up. "Ration what's in them as we need them.'

The chief nodded.

"Whew," commented Martin. "It wasn't something offensive."

I looked at him crossly.

"If you're in for the food run," the chief said, "we'll go tomorrow afternoon. It could be dangerous, but I need volunteers."

Myself, Avon, and four others raised our hands.

"I have a question," Martin spoke up. "Say, we go door to door. And people still don't shut down."

Another in the room spoke up, "Then it's their loss, their lives."

"Is it?" Martin asked. "I'm not affected, but if I play my music loud, blast my lights, and my neighbor who was in the dark dies, isn't that on me?" He looked to the chief. "Our actions can hurt others."

The chief nodded. "Yes, they can. And I have a plan B. I know those who don't power down put others in danger. If people don't ..." He shifted his eyes to me. "We hit the grid."

Avon interjected, "But it's not only lights. It's quiet, it's everything. How is getting everyone to go dark and quiet even going to be possible?"

"It'll be hard," the chief said. "But protecting lives until the danger has passed has to be our number one priority. If need be, to keep people alive, we will instill rules and enforce. We'll do what we need to do to protect people. By any means necessary." He paused. "Hopefully, it will not come to that."

Extreme measures were needed, I knew that.

I shuddered to think how far we would have to go to protect people.

Was it worth it?

If it wasn't for my mother would I be so willing to shut down and shut up?

Hopefully, everyone would do what was right. They'd turn off the lights, silence their lives, and do what was needed to protect themselves as well as others.

Be unselfish.

In the back of my mind, I knew that was probably just wishful thinking.

TWENTY-ONE
MYSTICAL

Day Five

Granted, growing up in Carthage had its advantages and disadvantages like any small town.

At some points, we were behind the times by choice.

Others, the world just passed us by until we caught up.

Some things were icons and I knew one of those technological gadgets from the past simply because our church held on to it.

"If it works, why replace it," the pastor would say.

I had forgotten about it until the next morning when the chief passed out the flyers for us to hand out and Martin took the stack, brought it to his nose and sniffed.

"Ah," Martin said. "Brings back memories."

The chief sniffed his stack. "Ditto. Makes me think of my friend Tim Suzchek. Back in the day, he volunteered at the church office to run the machine." He sniffed again.

Cody waved his finger. "You guys know you're sniffing methanol and isopropanol, right?"

"Okay," Martin replied in a 'what's your point' sort of way.

"Just making sure you know you're sniffing chemicals."

I had to ask, "Where did you get the machine from?"

"We had it. It was stored in records," the chief said. "Ironically, I found it the day I was down there when the flash happened. I thought this would be a better way than using the copier and the power."

Cody lifted his hand. "What time are we taking the truck?"

"Meet back here in three hours," the chief replied. "We'll walk out to Miller trucks to get it. Let's get these out there first, partner up and be careful."

We all turned to leave the back office and I watched Cody bring his stack to his nose. "Okay. I see why you guys do this."

I smiled. For a second, there was a blip of normalcy, one that wouldn't last.

We moved on with the buddy system, and while Cody asked to partner with me, and I would have preferred that, the chief thought it best that I partner with Avon.

Really?

The woman he didn't want to go because apparently there was something I was supposed to know about her that made her either unreliable or insane.

I was certain I'd learn what that was.

Making small talk, looking at the flyers.

They had been updated.

They not only asked people to power down, they told them what could happen and what to do, all in a neat bullet list fashion.

Our jobs were simple. We were to go door to door. We couldn't knock, we couldn't make a sound. Just stand and hope someone would see us, then leave the flyer.

Several homes we went to I could smell the burning.

I kept track of those houses.

Avon seemed nice enough. A little sad. For someone who interrupted the burial of my husband, suddenly she didn't have much to say.

So I asked.

"The chief insinuated I should know who you are," I said.

"I'm your neighbor."

"No." I shook my head. "As if I should know your name."

"You don't?" she asked.

"Nope. I mean you just moved here."

"I have lived here my entire life.'

"Really? I don't know you," I said.

"You don't know my name or story?"

I shook my head. "No, I don't."

"So you honestly weren't being insensitive or facetious yesterday?"

"I have no clue what you're talking about," I told her.

"My name is Avon Mersing."

"I know that."

"When I was a girl my entire family was abducted by aliens coming back from a camping trip."

I inhaled my gasp. It made sense, that was why everyone accused me of being offensive and insensitive. "Oh my god, that's you?"

"That's me."

"I remember hearing that story. The girl they found alone on the highway walking."

"Yes. I was just eleven."

"You know the story is your family just abandoned you and you concocted the alien story to make it less painful." I lifted my hand. "I'm not being insensitive, just saying what they said."

"They're wrong. My family was taken."

"And they didn't take you?" I asked.

"Oh they took me, they just gave me back."

"Really. Huh." I nodded. "You'll have to share details of that with me one day." I stopped as we approached Walt's house. "This should be easy. Walt's a hard guy to take, but he believes all kinds of stuff. Of everyone, he'll believe it."

Walt laughed.

He laughed hysterically.

"Get the hell out." He laughed again. "You expect people to believe this." He held the flyer, looked at it then sniffed it. "Dittos? Wow." He sniffed again.

"Yes, Walt," I said. "Because we're not using electricity."

"Because electricity, shock ..." he spat. "What else? Phones. Noise ..."

133

I added to his list. "Everything. Anything and everything can cause your internal system to …"

"Spontaneously combust?" he asked. "That isn't even real."

"It's not spontaneous combustion," I said. "It's your insides igniting."

Avon asked, "You haven't seen it? You haven't seen anyone do that?"

"George," Walt said. "He was lit by the grill."

"No." I shook my head. "It was the event.

Walt scoffed.

"Have you not paid attention?" Avon asked. "Twenty percent of this town is dead and more are going every day."

"Then maybe it's a plague or radiation from the event. But people aren't catching fire."

"What the hell is wrong with you?" I snapped. "You really think we'd be passing out these flyers if it wasn't true."

"I don't know." Walt shrugged. "I do know this. These flyers talk about anyone outside, right?"

"Yes." I nodded. "And those inside. But it happens slower to those inside."

"How do you prove it?" Walt asked.

Avon answered, "Marks. Everyone who was outside has burn marks. Some more than others but somewhere on their body are marks. Even those inside are getting them. The more they are exposed to the stimuli the more the marks appear."

"Is that so?" he asked. "I've been in my house, on my phone, playing video games with the AC on. I was out there looking up when the flash happened."

"Then you have marks," I said. "Let me see your arms."

He extended them both. I looked at them, lifting, turning, and checking under his tee shirt sleeves. Then I examined his neck.

Nothing.

"Can you lift your shirt?" I asked.

He did.

Not a mark on his stomach.

"Happy?" he asked. "Or do you want me just to take it all off in case I have the marks in strange areas."

"Yes, please," said Avon politely without batting an eye.

"What?" I asked. "No."

"Yes." She nodded. "He could have marks in unusual places."

Walter seemed amused. He took off every stitch of his clothing right there on his front porch. He lifted his arms and slowly turned clockwise.

Hating to admit it, I looked for marks on every part of his body I could see.

So did Avon.

Walt, with a smug look on his face, stood there in his naked glory and not a mark was on his body.

I knew for a fact he was out there ... exposed to the flash.

Nothing.

How was that possible?

TWENTY-TWO
CROWD CONTROL

Avon and I came across three people that claimed they were outside and had no marks. I mentioned it to Cody. He said he would love to run tests on them to see what caused the immunity if there was one.

Yeah, good luck getting Walt to agree to that.

Before leaving for the warehouse run, I made dinner. Cooking was a challenge. Eventually I'd run out of propane.

Cooking on an open fire was my next option.

A Coleman stove would have been better.

Myself, I would have been content with Ramen noodles, but my mother needed more and couldn't eat all that salt.

I used the last of the frozen meat which had thawed but not so much it went bad.

Meat, frozen stuff, none of that would be an option without power. We'd resort to hunting and fishing.

It wasn't for long. Only a month.

Had my mother been unexposed or not with us, I wouldn't be worrying about it. I would leave. Go with my daughter and wait it out.

Somewhere in the mountains, somewhere far away.

Not be a part of the craziness I knew would befall our town.

"What is the plan, Al?" my mother asked. "Really. You're going out and what?"

"There are only four of us plus the chief," I said. "We're taking a big truck from Millers and getting what we need from the food warehouse."

"Millers is two miles out," she said.

"I know. We're taking our bikes."

My mother nodded. "And the reason for getting the food."

"It won't be long before the store's shelves are wiped out. It won't be long before we will need that food. Each day that goes by it gets worse out there."

"So let it get worse," my mother commented. "Eventually everyone will die and there will be enough food."

"Mom."

"One truck will not do it, Al."

"Glad you're a survival expert. For now it will. We plan on hiding it until we need it," I replied.

"Where?" she asked.

"Miller's trucking."

"What does Mr. Miller say about that?"

I shrugged. "He died. Nothing really. His wife is fine with it."

"Mom," Sofie said sheepishly. "I hate that you're doing this. I'm scared for you. What if people out there are thinking the same thing? It's dangerous."

"I know."

"It's more dangerous for them if they were exposed," said my mother and she turned. "Don't go yet," she spoke as she walked away. "There's something I want you to take."

It was getting late, I needed to go. My mother returned with a small yellow case.

"What is it?" I asked.

"A stun gun."

"What?" I snatched it from her hand. "You can't have a stun gun. You're vulnerable."

"Exactly. It's the best weapon you can have right now," she said. "Make sure it's on and ready to use."

"Grandma," Sofie said. "Why do you have a stun gun?"

"Oh, I tried that Senior Silver dating site a couple years ago and never took it out of my purse since."

I clutched the case. "Thank you." My eyes moved to my mother's arms. She had a few burn marks. No new ones. "Mom, do they hurt? Be honest."

"Not like the burn I got on the air fryer," she replied. "It's weird, Al, it's like my muscles ache instead of my skin burning."

"That's good to know. Thank you. And thank you for the stun gun."

After putting it in my small backpack, and telling them not to wait up, I left the house.

A part of me really didn't worry about it being dangerous.

Was anyone but us really thinking ahead like that? As far as we knew, the rest of the world was in the dark.

The stun gun was a precaution.

Once outside and away from the house, I took it from the case and placed it in the waist of my pants.

Hopefully, I wouldn't need it.

Gordan came to my mind. Not that he wouldn't. I believed I loved him my entire life. We had a good relationship. We rarely fought in an angry manner, usually over dumb things.

It was hard to fathom that at the end of his life we were fighting. I never would have imagined that.

I was filled with sadness and guilt. Thinking about losing him crushed me in so many ways.

Making the store run, helping out in town was keeping my mind occupied.

I took my bike into town and when I pulled up to the station, I noticed a crowd outside the front door.

They were shouting, trying to get in, pounding on the door.

Yelling for the chief. They wanted answers. They screamed for the chief to talk to them.

I hopped off my bike, walking slowly as I passed them.

I could see only a few of them with burns. I thought of my mother and how she said the wounds didn't hurt. Not in a conventional way.

It made sense why people weren't seeking medical attention.

Still, they had to know the burns were a sign. Didn't they read the flyers we passed out?

Obviously they were there because of the flyer.

I shook my head as I passed them. "Are you guys stupid?" I asked. "You know you can like ignite and burst into flames at any second."

I guess I spoke those words louder than I thought. They stopped shouting and it seemed the entire crowd turned around and looked at me.

"Did you start this?" a man held a flyer. "Making people think stupid, unbelievable shit? I mean is this your way to cover for your daughter murdering George?"

"What?" I nearly laughed.

"Al," Avon approached and called my name softy. "Chief said come in the back."

"Oh. Oh," the same man commented. "Makes sense. Crazy loves crazy."

"That's not right," I replied. "You know what? Go ahead. Keep pounding on that door. In fact, why don't all of you pull out your cell phones, turn them one and make a call."

"Al," Avon said my name thought clenched jaws. "Come on."

"Yeah." I nodded and walked with her.

"They'll figure it out," Avon said. "When something seems impossible people disbelieve."

She knew that better than anyone.

As we walked toward the back of the building, I heard someone shout out. "Head to the back, that's where the chief is."

Another shouted, "He's hiding from us."

It was the strangest thing.

I heard them coming. The commotion, the shouting, the pounding feet.

The flyer wasn't meant to invoke such rage. But it did. Why? It simply asked people to power down and said why.

One would think they were being asked to give up all their worldly possessions.

Avon and I both picked up the pace, just wanting to get to the back.

I looked over my shoulder once to see the mob coming. I thought of that stun gun and about pulling it out. I dismissed that idea.

We weren't far from the back entrance, and Cody stood there holding the door.

We hadn't even crossed the threshold when I heard the scream.

I stopped running.

My eyes closed. I knew that cry.

The burning cry.

The scream was loud and shrill. One of pain and fear that didn't last long and was drowned out by the other cries from the mob.

Back tracking in my steps, I looked around the building. The crowd ran, but in the other direction, away from the station while the charred remains of one of them formed a smoldering pile on the ground.

No longer did they try to get to the chief.

I wondered if that was enough to convince them.

TWENTY-THREE
ROAD TRIP

We all grew silent with the same expression on our faces. At the back door, the five of us didn't move. Another death.

A senseless death.

I felt sick to my stomach. After the adrenaline of the moment passed, I just felt ill. I didn't even know who had fallen, who had burned.

"Do we know who that was?" I asked

"Mort Freeman," the Chief replied.

"It's only going to get worse," Cody said.

"It's the first time I saw that," Avon stated. "It's horrifying."

"Lucky you," I said. "I'm a magnet for this shit."

Snap.

Like some kind of Marvel movie moment, Cody snapped his finger, and we all were put on pause.

"That's it," Cody said.

We all looked at him.

"Sorry." He shook his head. "It just dawned on me why Walt may be immune to all of this."

"How?" I asked.

"He had that hip replacement last year."

"Okay." I shook my head confused.

"Just what you said about being a magnet for seeing this," Cody explained. "And I thought, I know for a fact Walt had a titanium hip put in and the joint has neodymium in it. Which is a magnet, which …"

"Really?" I snapped. "We had a mob out there. Someone died and you're thinking about Walt's hip."

"Sorry." Cody lifted his hand apologetically. "You're right." Silence.

"Barry Wright had a knee replacement," the chief said.

"Was he one of the immune?" Cody asked.

"Yeah, he is. You might be on to something."

I didn't get it. They were just changing subjects and talking nonchalantly as if a man they knew for years didn't just melt to the pavement.

It was time to go anyhow. Once we saw it was clear and no one was waiting outside we took our bikes and left town.

The highways were quiet, evening had set in and it started to get dark.

We didn't see a car on the road, not a single one.

When we arrived at Miller's we got a truck. It was good thing Martin knew how to drive a tractor trailer.

The chief sat up front. Cody, Avon, and I sat in the little sleeping area. I sat in the middle on a bed that didn't smell all that great.

The warehouse wasn't far and we slowed down as we approached.

We weren't the only ones with the idea to raid that warehouse.

The building had a glowing orange hue to it.

Four other trucks were there and one was in flames.

Did the occupants ignite or did the other trucks do it?

"What do you think?" Martin asked.

As soon as he said that, we saw four men approach the fence.

Cody leaned forward. "I'm thinking this isn't a good idea."

The chief looked back. "You're right. Martin, let's just back up."

"You got it, Chief." Martin shifted the gear and started backing up.

"Slow, so as not to alarm them," the chief said. "There's another warehouse ..."

The final word of 'south' trailed from the chief's lips as the driver's side of the windshield shattered when the first of several shots rang out.

"Get down!" the chief blasted. "Martin, drive. Go."

Another shot.

The chief grunted.

I could tell by the sound of his voice, the painful grunt that he was hit. Where I didn't know.

Suddenly, our truck moved fast in reverse, swerving back and forth. It felt like we were out of control.

We were.

Martin slumped to the wheel, his foot was still on the gas causing us to accelerate.

Groaning out, the chief reached over for Martin in some sort of vain attempt to stop the truck. Being center of the back bed seat, I leaped forward, reaching for Martin's leg as the chief reached for the steering wheel.

My grabbing his leg and the chief gripping the wheel caused Martin's body to fall on me.

I didn't have time to react, to do anything,

With a hard jolt I flew forward.

We not only stopped, we had crashed into something.

I had flipped a little, my back against the dash with Martin partially on top of me.

"Everyone ... everyone okay?" the chief asked.

Hearing him ask was a sign of relief. He wasn't fatally injured. At least I hoped he wasn't.

It took everything I had to lift Martin even a little from me. He wasn't a big man, but the weight was heavy. I caught a glimpse of his face. Eyes wide open, part of his forehead missing. Then he rolled down to the floor of the truck.

I twisted and turned trying to get out from under him.

There wasn't a lot of room and as I wiggled, the stun gun popped out from the waist of my pants.

I reached for it. Ironically I did so at the same time the chief's door opened.

A man was there.

All I could see of him was his head, chest and the rifle he held.

He was close enough to me that I could see his face was splattered with burn marks.

He aimed at the chief.

But I fired.

I swung around the stun gun and pressed the trigger.

A quick depression, that was all that was needed.

Strands of blue electrical current flew from the budget store taser and hit into the man with the rifle.

As I suspected, the voltage didn't shock him. Like the AED, it caused an ignition and following a brief scream, the man erupted into flames.

His arms swung wildly as he stepped back. He moved in a fiery state of panic but only for a few seconds before his entire being crumpled and dropped to the ground.

Another man jumped forward to the door and I did the same to him, without hesitation.

The adrenaline of that moment pumped through my system.

So much noise. So much going on.

Cody yelled, "No."

Avon screamed. She screamed over and over.

The chief breathed heavily, holding on to his side which bled profusely.

I wasn't thinking about anything but surviving.

Perhaps that was why I fired again when the third man appeared at the door.

He went down like the others, a crumbled decimated body.

Then no more came.

There were more out there, I knew it. Where were they?

The interior of the truck drew quiet with the exception of Avon's soft weeping.

Breathing heavily, I was on the floor sandwiched between a dead body and the chief.

Was it over?

It was not how I imaged the night to go.

What part of me realistically believed we would ride our bikes to Millers, drive to the warehouse and easily walk away with what we needed?

My daughter was right when she said, *What if people out there are thinking the same thing? It's dangerous.*

It was dangerous and people had the same idea.

My whole body felt numb and I couldn't move.

Not only was I certain I was in a state of shock, I was also certain I wasn't sure how much more I could take.

TWENTY-FOUR
AVON'S STORY

The world was the new wild, wild west and I was an outlaw. Although I doubted outlaws felt guilt and I did.

I had killed three men.

Without hesitancy, without thought.

Done. Dead.

Three. How would I manage to close my eyes at night, without carrying that with me? If asked a week earlier if I had the ability to take three lives, I would have said I didn't. I couldn't even kill a bug.

Yet, I fired at will.

What was wrong with me?

Emotionally I was disheveled and on the floor of our truck, I couldn't move.

Cody sprang into action.

He grabbed the stun gun from my hand. "Help Craig," he said, just before climbing over Martin's body and out the door.

I was so out of it, I almost asked who Craig was then I realized he meant the chief. Taking care of him was hard to do. I was afraid to get up from that floor, even just a little.

"It's okay," the chief said through a strained voice. "I don't think it's too bad."

"Where are you hit?"

"Here."

Lifting my eyes I saw the blood pouring from the wound around his lower left ribcage.

I placed my hand tight against it to give pressure, to stop the bleeding. At first I felt the warm blood hit against the palm of my hand, then the flowing blood lessened.

I kept the pressure tight.

Where did Cody go? What was he doing?"

"There's a first aid kit back here," Avon said. "It's small."

"I doubt there's anything in there."

"Where's Doctor Dogan?" she asked.

"I don't know." My head turned sharply to the sound of the scream in the distance. A short scream and I hoped it wasn't Cody.

"Here." Avon handed me a tee shirt. It was very large and probably belonged to the man who drove the truck. "There are no large bandages."

"I didn't think so." I took the shirt and hurriedly placed it under my hand. "How are you doing, Chief?"

"I'm okay."

After a few minutes of silence, my hand pressed against the wound, Cody appeared at the chief's open door.

I sighed out in relief. "You're okay."

"Yeah, yeah, I am," he said nervously. "Craig, can you walk?"

The chief nodded. "I think so yeah."

"Are you nuts?" I asked. "He can't walk all the way back home."

"He doesn't need to," Cody said. "He only needs to get a hundred feet."

A hundred feet?

I was confused.

"Is it safe?" I asked.

"Yes, it's safe," Cody replied. "We need to get him to a hospital and fast."

With Cody's help, the chief nearly rolled from the truck, then Avon and I climbed out.

Cody helped the chief to walk. The chief's arm slung over Cody's shoulder and he leaned on the smaller medical examiner as they walked toward the fence.

A truck was near the open gate, the driver's door open, headlights on and it looked as if it were leaving. There were other trucks. Two inside the fenced in area.

The threat was over.

Another three piles of smoldering flesh were around the fence.

Rifles, backpacks were by those piles.

"Pick up the weapons and the packs," Cody told me. "We'll take all we can get."

It was a lot, but Avon and I did. As we walked by, we grabbed what we could.

As I suspected, Cody helped the chief in the truck by the fence.

It wasn't as big as the truck we had.

"Back end is open," Cody said. "You and Avon squeeze back there. I'll drive. I'll give you your stun gun when we stop. Pound on the truck when you're in and ready."

I wasn't sure if I even wanted the gun back. Cody didn't need to tell me what he did. I saw it.

He found his way to quickly eliminate the threat.

Duffle bags, backpacks hanging over our shoulders, Avon and I were bogged down as we made it to the back of the truck.

The back gate was rolled up and as I went to toss my items inside I saw the hand.

An undamaged female hand with perfect maroon nail polish on the fingers. Near that hand was a handgun and by that were partial remains.

Not ashes like most. But bits and pieces of charred body parts. It looked as if she shattered.

We climbed inside with the items. My eyes staying on the woman's remains.

Part of a blue shirt, a gold band, purple Fitbit were recognizable.

Inside, Avon did something I didn't expect.

Using one of the large duffle bags she shoveled the remains out of the back of the truck. As they landed to the ground a plume of ashes rose and I cringed.

There were boxes in there, marked with various food items. Big five-gallon bottles of water.

I couldn't think about what I had just witnessed. We had to go.

After pounding on the side of the truck, I closed the gate.

We moved quickly. I had to hold on with every turn.

"Are you alright?" Avon asked.

"Yeah. You?"

"I've been through worse."

Through worse? That just seemed insane to me.

I couldn't see where we were going, there were no windows. But I knew we arrived at the hospital when the truck stopped.

At least I hoped.

After hearing the door open, I raised the gate.

It was nighttime, the sun had set and the automatic street lamps of the hospital parking lot were on.

Avon and I climbed out. Cody had already retrieved a gurney and pushed it to the truck.

The entire outside of the emergency room entrance was lit up and welcoming.

At first glance it was normal, but it wasn't.

No one was around.

No one alive that was.

Avon helped Cody get the chief on the gurney and I just looked around.

Charred remains were outside. It had happened fast. There was still a cigarette burning in the astray.

"Cody," I said. "No one is here to help."

"We don't know that," he replied.

"Yeah, Cody we do." My voice quivered and we all pushed the gurney through the automatic doors.

We were greeted with water as it poured from the sprinkler system. A strobe light flashed and the fire alarm blared.

Smoke lingered in the waiting room.

Not a soul was there.

If power, electricity, and noise truly were the catalyst, then the brightly lit hospital wasn't the place to be.

Cody never flinched. He stayed calm, cool, and pushed the chief into the back triage area.

It was a crash course in emergency medicine for both Avon and I. Running about looking for things that he needed.

Two hours later, Cody was able to retrieve the bullet from inside the chief, stabilize him, and hook him to an IV.

He would be alright. Cody was confident. But he didn't want to leave the chief. At least for a few hours.

"Take the truck," Cody told me. "Hide it at Millers. When Craig is strong enough I'll push him in a wheelchair back to town. I don't want to roll the truck through town."

I understood that.

I wished the chief good luck, then Avon and I took the truck.

Never had I driven anything that big or heavy, but I managed. There were no other cars on the road.

As instructed we left the truck at Miller's and grabbed our bikes.

We rode for a little bit, but my legs felt like rubber. I was an emotional mess and in the quiet night, everything just pounded at me.

So we walked our bikes the final mile.

"The chief will be alright," Avon said. "If anyone can save a life it's someone that knows how people die."

"I never thought of it like that," I replied. "I agree though. You're very strong, Avon."

"So you are you."

"Maybe I don't see it, but you don't seem half as much the mess as I am. Look at my hand." I lifted my hand to show her how badly I trembled.

"I'm just really good at hiding it. I'm a mess," she said. "You know this is the road it happened. Not far from here."

"What?" I asked.

"The abduction."

I didn't know how I had forgotten, but Gordan brought up the Avon incident once or twice. Probably in passing, maybe it was after the Easter tradition of watching the movie *Independence Day*, but he brought her up.

"Right here on this road?" I asked.

She nodded. "It was early morning. The sun wasn't up. We were headed to Yellowstone for vacation. I remember the bright lights coming over the horizon. My mom ... she thought it was a truck. She yelled 'Jesus, Joe, the truck is gonna hit us.'"

"You heard that?"

"Yeah. I thought it was a truck, too. Then the whole car got bright."

"Did you black out and wake up on the road? I know it's been said they found you walking alone."

Avon shook her head. "Not entirely. My father stopped the car. Was questioning what it was. The light grew brighter and there was this loud squealing noise. I blacked out. But just for a second. I woke up on the ship."

"A space ship."

"Yes. I could see my parents on a table by me. My brother. My mother was screaming. They were trying to put something in her mouth. It was dark, a few flashes of light in there."

"What did they look like?" I asked.

"They were shaped like you and I. Only they had these spacesuits on."

"Jesus."

"I know, right?" she said.

"How did you escape? Or don't you remember?"

"I don't remember. I think they let me go. I just know I was running down the road when they found me."

"I'm sorry, Avon, I really am."

"It's okay."

"No, I'm sorry for that and for all that you have endured." I looked at her. So innocent. She truly believed what happened and who was I to question?

We had talked so much, the walk to town had flown by.

It was the sounds of firetruck sirens that brought me back to reality.

As we hit the edge of town, there was a glow that hung over our dark town. When I saw that, I got a sickening feeling in my gut.

"Maybe we should ride our bikes," I suggested.

We both hopped on, and before we could even peddle, a fire truck zoomed by us.

It sent a chill up my spine.

All that noise, the commotion. How many people would pay the price?

Didn't they see what caused it? What was going on? The fire department was only doing their job.

I got that.

As we rode down the main street, half the businesses had lights on. The police station was the darkest building.

What would it take for things to change?

Every day was going to be a crap shoot of who would burn next. How many would ignite.

Did people think they could just keep living their lives and nothing would change?

It was the moment we turned on our street that I knew, no matter how hard I tried to follow the rules, things would keep happening to me.

I prayed and begged God when I saw the fire trucks on our street.

"Please don't let it be my house. Please."

Then I saw my daughter.

Sofie staggered a run to me. And I hoped off my bike, letting it fall as I rushed to her.

"Mommy," she cried desperately. "Oh, Mommy."

"Baby what is it?"

Sofie grabbed on and clutched me. "Mommy ... Grandma's dead."

TWENTY-FIVE
DONE, JUST DONE

Everything I did was for my mother.

I absolutely cared about the town, but I would not have been so adamant about powering down, passing out those flyers, going on a dangerous food run if I didn't want my mother protected.

Every single measure was for her … now she was dead.

Was the courage and strength I felt the previous couple of days a ruse? Just a passing thing? Was I fooling myself into believing I was strong?

Some sort of Liam Neeson in an apocalyptic world. One dangerous thing after another. Only I didn't win.

At first when Sofie told me, I was in shock. Complete disbelief. No way. I didn't believe it. Even though the top floor of my house had been gutted with flames, I didn't believe it.

It was continuous death. One right after another.

Friends, people I knew, people I tolerated, and those I loved.

Gone in a flash … literally.

What happened with my mother?

Jan burned in a bed and her house was fine.

My mother didn't just flame out she took the house with her.

It made me think something else happened, maybe it wasn't her igniting.

I didn't think too far into it because it didn't matter. My mother was gone.

I loved my mother to death, she didn't deserve what happened to her. She didn't deserve the pain and suffering.

My family.

My husband and mother both taken from us tragically.

"We went to bed, Mommy," Sofie said. "We were fine. I heard the smoke alarm and … I couldn't help her. I couldn't get near her."

I whispered a comforting "Shh," pulling her closer.

Cody had given us hope that if we kept everyone quiet and away from anything that could spark them, they would be fine.

Death by ignition wasn't supposed to be inevitable if we did everything we were supposed to.

Apparently, that was wrong.

I stood on the sidewalk watching the fire department put out the flames. They were so heroic.

Most of them from what I could see were suffering the effects from the event, yet they still worked to put out the flames.

The right side of my roof was gone. I couldn't see any more flames. Just the mist of smoke from the cold water against the hot burning wood.

We stood on the sidewalk for hours. A crowd was there at first. Watching the burning house as if it were some sort of entertainment.

But as the flames died, the crowd left.

All but Avon.

I held on to my daughter and Avon stood near us. I don't think it was out of support, more so because they wouldn't let her go into her house ... just in case.

"I'm so sorry, Al," Avon said. "I am."

She was.

Her condolences were genuine.

A few firefighters were in my house. They moved about, I could see the dancing beams of their flashlights.

Then the fire chief approached me.

I had known Daryl since grade school. His father was a firefighter and so were his grandfather and brother.

"Sorry, Al," he said. "You have my sympathies."

"I know this question is in vain, but did you find her?"

He shook his head. "We'll see better in the morning. I doubt we will find any remains."

I nodded. I wondered if he knew what was going on? I wondered if he knew that the marks on his body meant his death sooner than later.

"We don't know exactly what is causing this phenomenon," he said. "It's a pandemic. It's crazy, it's every day, every night."

"I saw what happened to my husband, my neighbors. The house ... didn't burn."

"Not usually. We have had several that did," he explained. "The room caught on fire as well. Not many but it has happened. Depends on where they are in the room, what they are wearing. We found the burned remains of a tablet next to the window. I think when she caught on fire, she ignited the curtains."

That made sense.

The tablet.

She probably stood by the window trying to get a signal.

Daryl placed his hand on my arm. "Again, I'm sorry. We'll be back in the morning to assess."

"Thank you."

"Do you have somewhere to go tonight?" he asked.

Avon spoke up. "They can stay with me. You're welcome to stay with me."

"I know this is probably easier said than done," Daryl said. "But try to get some rest."

He walked away and back to the truck.

"I'll go over and start the Coleman stove," Avon said. "I'll make us some dinner. I know you're hungry."

My voice cracked as I stammered out a, "Thank you."

I stayed on the sidewalk until the last of the firefighters left and my house was just a dark, dismal empty shell of life.

The walk over to Avon's house wasn't far but each step I took, I thought of everything I had endured.

All those that died.

The horrors I witnessed.

My poor Gordan.

162

My mother.

The three men I killed without batting an eye.

The world was insane now.

When we arrived at her house, Avon had a candle on the outdoor dining table on the back patio. It was set for a late dinner of soup and crackers. She handed me a glass of wine. I needed it.

I didn't feel much like eating, but she went to all that trouble and I appreciated it. Sofie and I would eat.

"I know I told you before," Avon said. "But I am sorry. Sofie, I am sorry."

"Thank you," I replied. "We appreciate your help." I alternated between the soup and the wine then finally, I downed my drink, and she quickly refreshed the glass.

"I have more wine and harder stuff if you want." Avon placed down the bottle. "Just know, my home is your home. You can stay here as long as you want."

"Thank you. But it won't be necessary."

Sofie asked, "Are we gonna go to Grandma's house?"

I shook my head. "Nope. Tonight, we rest. Tomorrow we salvage what we can, get some food and we go. We're leaving."

I saw the confusion on both of their faces. They didn't know what I meant or was talking about. I'd explain it when I knew exactly what the plan was.

I knew one thing. There was no reason for me to stay in town, to fight to save lives because the last person I loved was gone. Now I had to worry about my daughter.

With all that was happening, I wanted to take her. Get her as far away from people and the craziness as I could. Stay away until it was over. As long as that would be.

I couldn't stay in town, near my home or my mother's house.

I couldn't stay around anyone.

I was done.

TWENTY-SIX
DEPENDS

Day Six

My life fell apart in less than a week.

At least I still had Sofie. We did more than fold laundry that fateful day in the Dillard basement. We formed a survivor bond.

We were different. We weren't in danger from electronics, or anything like that. I feared the longer we remained fine we were in danger from those who would resent us.

That played a factor into my decision for us to go.

To leave.

Eventually things would stop. The affected would die out or get better, but it would end.

We just had to wait it out.

I wanted to take everything from my home, but I kept telling myself I could come back.

That was until I walked back into my home after the fire.

The flames had taken away the second floor but the water damage destroyed everything else.

It smelled like a campfire after rain.

Our feet splashed in the water that formed on the floors. Furniture was toppled. We took what pictures we could, enough to keep memories alive, then we went into the kitchen.

Part of the ceiling was gone and the sun peaked through. The kitchen cabinets were covered in a muddy soot.

The labels were tearing off the canned goods and any boxed food was useless unless it was sealed in plastic.

We spent a good hour going through the supplies.

"Do you know where we're going?" Sofie asked.

"Yeah, I do," I told her. "It won't be easy, but it's what we have to do. I promise you, we'll manage. It won't be long. Just until it's over."

"How will we know when it's over?" Sofie asked.

"Look how fast people are dying, honey. It won't take long."

She whimpered some and lowered her head. "I don't want to leave our home."

"I know. But I can't be around any more death. We just need to go."

"But we're safe," she said. "It won't happen to us."

"I know. But what happens when people realize that. No, it's for the best."

"Where?" she asked. "Where are we going?"

"I thought run for the hills ... literally. Go off grid. Hit a wooded area ..."

"The reserve," Avon's voice entered the kitchen. "I'm sorry, I came over to check on you. I heard you talking. Go to the reserve in Stockton. You can fish. There are cabins all over the place up there."

"That's seventy miles," I said.

"Drive," she replied. "We can drive. We don't have to worry about the car hurting us ..."

"Wait." I held up my hand. "We?"

"I want to go with you. I need to get out of the insanity and it's only going to get worse," she said. "I have fishing gear from my husband. Rifles. And I have food."

I shook my head. "I don't know."

"Mom," Sofie said. "She can't be alone either."

"I know the area well," said Avon. "Please. Please let me go with you."

Even if Avon didn't know the area as well as she claimed, just the shear amount of food in her house made her a valuable asset.

I worried about how to carry it all.

If those men were an indication on how desperate people were getting for food, we were in trouble.

I'd figure that part out once we finished organizing what we had. We did so at Avon's kitchen table.

Anything in boxes that could be removed, we did so for space. We fit three pounds of uncooked spaghetti in a plastic storage bag.

Center of the table next to the huge unopened jar of mayonnaise was an even larger unopened jar of peanut butter.

Sofie lifted it. "This is a big jar for just two people."

"We love peanut butter," said Avon. "We buy a jar of month and trust me we are scraping the bottom of it."

Sofie whistled. "That's a lot of peanut butter."

"Everyday one of us, if not both, were digging in."

"You know"—I waved my finger—"that is good to know. I think we're going to have to be gone for at least a month. Knowing this is a month's worth is helpful."

"You know," Avon said, "have you thought about how we're going to hide this in the car? We can take my SUV and take more. But we still need to figure out how to hide it and carry some if we have to walk."

"Why would we have to walk?" Sofie asked.

Avon shook her head. "You have to think of every possible outcome. I learned that early on. My husband was one of those couch survivalists."

Sofie looked at her curiously. "What is that? A couch ... survivalist?"

"Learns everything he can about survival, thought he knew it all," Avon replied. "Only went halfway with applying that knowledge."

Sofie shook her head. "No, he didn't. I bet any money you know exactly what do to."

"Maybe, huh?"

"You're already talking about hiding food. That's smart. And you have a lot." Sofie's hand paused while sorting noodles. "What about your brother? The sun guy? Are you gonna go find him?"

Avon shook her head. "Not right now. He lives in Canada. He said when it's safe he will find me. I don't expect him to. He's my foster brother. He may." She shrugged it off. "He said leave a note in the toilet tank if I leave."

"In plastic I hope," Sofie said.

"In plastic."

Sofie turned to me. "Mom? Do you feel bad about leaving everyone in town?"

"No," I answered without hesitation. "Why?"

"They're your neighbors. They're sick," Avon said. "What if they run out of food like this?"

"Sweetie, that is not my problem."

"You started making it your problem," Sofie said. "I'm just wondering."

Avon answered, "I think your mom was only doing it for her mom which, to me, was reason enough." She looked at me. "I'm sorry, I don't want to speak for you."

"It's fine.'

"Are you alright?" Avon reached out touching my arm. "Do you need anything?"

"No, I'm okay. Maybe some ideas on where to hide the food."

"I read in a book once," Avon said. "In the spare tire compartment. Oh!" She snapped her fingers. "I've got an idea."

Avon stopped what she was doing, scurried out of the kitchen and in a few seconds returned with a large adult diaper box.

"There's an entire package left." She lifted it from the box. "We can put the food in the box and cover it with the Depends. They'll open the lid and not touch it."

I chuckled a little. "Yes, they would."

"I wouldn't," Sofie said.

"It's like hiding money in a tampon box," Avon stated. "When I was in foster care, I always hid things in my feminine protection boxes."

"This is a really good idea," Sofie said. "Why do you have them?" She gasped. "Oh my gosh, I'm sorry, that was personal."

Avon smiled gently. "No, it's fine. It's from when Roy, my husband, his grandmother lived here. What a crazy time. I'm sure you remember."

"Oh," Sofie said knowingly. "Yeah, I remember that. It was."

I shook my head. "I don't. You do?"

Sofie nodded. "Yeah."

"You don't remember?" Avon asked. "I mean the chief was here all the time. She'd wander into people's houses."

"Naked," Sofie added. "She was always naked except her boots."

"What?" I asked. "Really?"

"You don't remember?" Sofie asked. "Daddy always helped find her or helped get her back in the house."

"Daddy did?" I asked.

Sofie nodded.

"I'm sorry. Where was I? Wait. Don't answer." I lifted my hand.

I didn't need an answer. I was in my own world. If I didn't notice a naked senior citizen running around and being chased by the police, was it any wonder why I would walk away from my town?

"Hello?" Cody's voice called from outside "I'm looking for Al."

"In here," I replied.

I heard him open the door. He wiped his feet and stepped inside. "Al," he said and rushed to me. "I am so sorry. I just heard. I am sorry. My home is open to you and your daughter."

"Thank you," I replied. "How's the chief?"

"Good. Craig is strong. I have no doubt he'll be back at the station tonight ..." He looked at the table. "What's going on?"

"We're gathering supplies," I said.

"Good, that's good. Make sure you hide them, though."

"We're leaving, Cody," I told him. "We're leaving town. Heading to the proverbial hills to wait this out."

"Wait? What?" Cody said shocked. "You can't leave."

"Yes, I can."

"No, Al, you're part of the team. We need you to help the people in this town. There are so few of us. We have an obligation ..."

"I have an obligation to my child. To keep her safe."

"And you think running to the hills will do that?" Cody asked.

"A lot easier than here. The people in this town are not my obligation."

"They were last night," he said.

"No, Cody, my mother was my obligation last night. Now she is gone. She was the sole reason I wanted to bring silence and dark here. To make this a quiet world. For her. Now that doesn't matter. And you can't stop people from dying. No matter how hard you try, no matter what you do, they are gonna ignite. Why? Because they don't think it will happen to them. Just like my mother."

"Okay. Okay." Cody lifted his hands. "I get it. I do. You've been through a lot."

I huffed out a sarcastic laugh.

"Just think about what all happened last night. Everything that happened," he said. "Give it a day."

"What does a day mean?" I asked.

"It means one day to think about it. Please, give us one day. It's easy to run when you're scared or hurt. To do so without thought. I am only asking you to think about it. Wait one day, think about it and plan it out," Cody said. "Maybe you'll change your mind. You and Sofie aren't in danger of igniting. You're safe here. Out there you don't know. You saw that last night. In here, in town you're safe. Think of your daughter."

"I am," I replied.

"Then think a little longer."

I felt pressured, cornered. Why did Cody even stop by? Didn't he see or realize all I was dealing with?

After muttering, "Excuse me, I need air," I stepped away from the table and the house, walking outside.

As soon as I did, I saw my home.

Destroyed. Gone.

There would be no insurance company to send an adjuster. For the rest of time, my house would be a burned monument to all that happened, all I had lost.

I shuddered and fought the tears. My losses weighed me down. My entire soul felt too heavy to bear. Arms tightly folded to my body, I walked. I kept walking.

A block then two … On my walk I saw piles of remains on the street. Ashes slightly blowing in the wind.

Sirens blared in the distance. How much longer would the firefighters battle the blazes? How much longer would the emergency workers keep showing up?

How long would they live?

I didn't know where I was going, or why. I just felt the need to run. Much like how I was feeling about getting out of town.

There was no destination or intention to stop. But I did. I stopped dead in my tracks when I saw it.

It was also at that moment I realized Cody was following me.

I stood there on the sidewalk staring across the street. A sickening knot in my stomach.

I recognized two things.

The red wagon and the Weston Funeral Home shirt.

Lying on the sidewalk by the wagon was the young man that had brought me Gordan's ashes.

I crossed the street.

He had been dead long enough for the odor to carry my way. He lay on his stomach, his face drawn of all color, and his cheeks dark where they pressed on the sidewalk. A single bullet hole was in his forehead and another in his chest.

The wagon had three little boxes of remains.

My heart broke for him. It really did. He had nothing but people in his wagon, why would someone do that to him?

"Al," Cody called my name softly. "Don't look."

"No, we need to look. He wasn't exposed, Cody. He told me. This poor man. If you want to know why I am leaving, this is more than enough reason." I pointed to him. "He was doing a job to help the people in this town and this is what happened to him. We're not safe, Cody, me and Sofie are not safe here. He wasn't."

"If you aren't safe here, you won't be safe anywhere," Cody said.

"I think we stand a better chance buried in the woods," I said, then faced him. "I'll stay one more day. See the chief, make sure we aren't running off half-cocked. Get our plan together. Maybe find his mom." I pointed to the Weston man. "Finish what he started."

"See, Al, you saying that tells me you care. This town needs you," Cody stated. "It needs your help."

"He tried to help the town. Look where it got him. What could he possibly have done? Nothing. People are going crazy. I can't, Cody, I can't stay. For the sake of my daughter, for her life, I have to run. I'm sorry."

I really was sorry for Cody, for not being able to be the help he needed. But I couldn't stay in town, I couldn't take a chance that my daughter would be the next person to be the recipient of an attack. An 'If I'm dying, I'm taking you with me' sort of thing.

As I told Cody I would stay one more day. Give myself enough time to make sure we did things right when we left.

Then we'd go. And if I came back it wouldn't be until it was done and over with.

TWENTY-SEVEN
LEAVING

Day Seven

His name was Landon Pierce. He was twenty-four years old and had only worked at Weston for seven months. He graduated Mortuary School not a year earlier.

He lived at home with his father and mother. I found them. They were buried in the backyard with a grave marker similar to the one I made Gordan.

He lost both his parents and kept working.

He kept going.

Maybe it was to keep his mind occupied and away from the pain.

I got Cody and Daryl and they helped me bury the young man right by his parents. Then I finished delivering the final remains.

No one was home to claim them.

I set them on the porch of the respective homes.

I learned about Landon not because anyone told me but by his employee records at Weston.

Weston was a nightmare.

The last time I was there, lines of people had formed outside. But when I returned, everyone was gone. A few piles of remains were on the sidewalk.

If it rained, they'd be gone too.

Weston Funeral Home had been long since abandoned. No workers there. Scores of charred remains were on tables and gurneys.

The kilns were cold.

No bodies had been cremated for a while. Landon took what remained and stayed busy.

That poor boy.

Quietly, pulling the empty wagon, I headed back to my home.

We were packed and ready to go. Our plan was to drive the SUV slowly to the highway and head northeast.

The only problem that I foresaw was the two towns we had to pass through. I would look at the map thoroughly to find a way around them, avoid people. Not just for our safety but for theirs as well.

I made one more promise and that was to stop and see Cody and the chief before I left.

The town changed overnight. It grew quiet. Yet, trails of smoke rose to the sky from all over.

The body count increased daily.

177

Didn't they see? Didn't they understand? They needed to just stop and shut down. However, technology was addictive. No one willingly wanted to be in the dark. No power, no fans or refrigerators.

My mother proved my point, she honestly didn't think being online for a minute would kill her.

It did.

I saw no one on the street, no businesses open. It was weird, eerie.

The door to the police station was propped open, probably to let some air in. It was already warm and it wasn't even noon.

When I stepped in, Cody was in there with the chief. The chief looked good. He looked well and that made me feel better.

Cody sat on the desk, looking over his shoulder at me. "You're leaving."

"I am."

The chief asked. "You'll come back?"

"I will, yes, this is my home."

Cody nodded. "Can I ask where you're going?"

"To the reserve. Find a cabin. Stay there," I answered.

"One month, Al," Cody said. "One month, that's all you need. Six weeks if you want to be safe and sure, but in four weeks, people will be healing."

I shook my head. "They can't heal if they won't let go."

"Of power? Internet?" the chief asked. "They don't have a choice now. Yesterday, those who were still online found out the truth. Pretty much confirming what Cody has told us. Folks took the news seriously. The grid was hit last night."

Cody added, "Someone wanted to make sure things stayed dark.'

"Wasn't me." I lifted my hand. "I swear."

"Oh, we know," the chief said. "There were remains out there. Jenkins, God rest his soul, found them."

God rest his soul.

A knot formed in my stomach when I heard that. "I saw a lot of smoke, Chief. A lot of people died last night, I take it."

The chief nodded. "They did. Some people are and were too far gone. There's no healing, no turning back."

"What are they saying?" I asked. "Or what did they say?"

"They said everything was to be shut down. That no cars, no electricity, nothing. Quiet," the chief said. "They said that's what people need to do."

"We know," Cody said, "there will be people who won't believe. I spoke to a friend in London. The international community that was in the dark when the flash hit, they can't send aid for a month. They can't take a chance of any disturbance over here. They have people on the ground here, observing, learning."

"So there are unaffected scientists here?" I asked. "That's good to know."

"Another thing," the chief said. "The final broadcast announced that there were people not affected. Those below, in the subway, any place without a window and they were imploring those people to help."

"Are you telling me this to get me to stay?" I asked.

The chief shook his head. "No, I'm telling you this to be careful. I think that there will be a lot of resentment attacks on those not affected. It's bound to happen."

"It did happen," I said. "Landon from Weston funeral home."

The chief nodded. "I think what you are doing is the best choice. Stay safe. Protect your child. But listen to me, let no one ... no one know you weren't affected. Got that?"

"Even if you have to burn yourself," said Cody.

"What?" I asked with a sarcastic chuckle.

"We're serious," the chief said. "Let no one know. It's the same thing as not letting someone know how much food or water you have."

"Okay ... I'll make sure we appear like everyone else. But I don't think we'll run into anyone," I said. "We're going straight there."

"Good. Just please be careful," the chief said.

"I will."

"I wish you weren't going," Cody stated. "We could find a way to keep you safe."

"It's more than that," I told him. "I can't watch another person I know die. I just can't. That's why the three of us are taking off."

"Three?" the chief asked. "Tell me Avon is not going with you."

"She is."

"Al, she is not in her right mind. She never has been."

"And with good reason," I rebutted. "If she was not in her right mind, then how did she keep a husband for so long? Huh?"

"Who knows?" the chief shrugged. "I just know she isn't right."

"Is she dangerous?" I asked.

The chief shook his head. "No."

"Unstable isn't good," said Cody. "Her husband had her committed many times because she kept having ..." He paused to do air quotes. "Flashbacks of her abduction."

"How do all you people know everyone's business in this town but me?" I asked. "And who are we to say she wasn't abducted as a child? Because you don't believe in aliens. We don't know."

"We do," said the chief. "Did she tell you her story?"

"Yes." I nodded. "She was with her family, on the highway, they saw the bright light. She woke up in the spaceship. Her family was being experimented on by people in spacesuits. Then the next thing she knew she was walking on the highway."

"That story is a bit twisted around," the chief said. "That was only seventeen years ago, I was on the force. I remember it well. Because I was the one that found her. I found her wandering the highway, scared, confused, and bloody."

"And her family gone."

"Just about. They weren't abducted," he said. "I've heard her story a million times. Her family was around her. She twisted the story in her mind. The wandering the highway came before seeing her family experimented on."

"I don't understand."

"Her family wasn't abducted. A tractor trailer carrying chemicals crashed into their car. Avon was thrown. She was injured and confused. I found her walking. She was in the emergency room with her family. The space suits were the hazmat suits because of the chemicals. They died, Al, her family all died that night by her."

"But she believes she was abducted," I said.

"She wasn't."

"That makes her crazy?" I asked.

"Well ..."

"No." I stopped the chief. "No, it doesn't. It makes her a survivor. She believed what she had to believe to make survival easiest. She did what she had to do, just like we're doing now. And you know what, Craig? I wish to God I could believe my mom or Gordan were taken by aliens instead of knowing how horribly they died."

"I understand," the chief said humbly.

"Do you?" I asked.

"I do."

"I don't know much about Avon," I said. "That's my fault. I lived next door to her and never bothered to meet her. But she's a good soul. I feel it. She's not a danger, so what's the difference?"

"You're right."

"That was easy." I smiled slightly. "I'll be back. I'll come home. I promise."

"If not," the chief said, "we'll come looking for you."

A part of me really, truly hated leaving my town, leaving the chief and Cody to fend for themselves and do all that needed to be done.

But I had to do what needed to be done.

That was protect my child.

While it was a moral responsibility to do my part, I couldn't. I just couldn't.

Was it cowardly to leave? Maybe.

I didn't care.

I'd lost so much, witnessed horrors and I reached my end.

Broken and beaten, I had no other choice.

I needed to get me and my daughter away from it all. Run. Hide. Whatever it took to make it through.

And we would.

TWENTY-EIGHT
NEW WORLD UP THE ROAD

We were packed up.

By my estimate, even if we never fished or hunted, we had enough food for six weeks. No, we had plenty.

Using Avon's logic, we hid a third of our supplies in the car. Removing the spare tire, we hid a ton of dry goods in the wheel holder. The Depends adult undergarment box perched on that.

Behind the rear seat of her SUV was this strange felt material that enabled the back seat to be laid flat. We removed it, put supplies in there and sealed it back up.

The rest we had in duffle bags, backpacks, and boxes.

We left under different conditions than we anticipated. When we went to sleep the night before, the world knew nothing or maybe didn't believe what was happening.

Now we ventured out into a world that knew, was scared, and desperate to live.

All the more reason to head to the hills.

It was sixty-seven miles to the reserve.

The first third of the trip I didn't worry about. It was the interstate north and we'd travel that without any problem. It was when we headed east on the state road.

A road that went back and forth from two lanes to four, but more so, it went directly through two towns just before the backroads to the Stockton Reserve.

That worried me.

Two towns we had to go through.

Looking at the map, I saw a way around. Two miles before the first small town, we'd go south, take the long way around the outskirts.

That was the plan.

The highway was just as I thought it would be. A few cars here and there, nothing in our way. Smooth sailing to the State Road. I thought all was good. We were in the clear.

"Looks like a traffic light," Avon said. "Right before the town. That's the right you want to make."

"How far out of the way will it take us?" Sofie asked.

"Total four miles, but it'll keep us away from people."

Or so I thought.

Then not even another quarter of a mile, just before that traffic light at the Dollar Value store was a roadblock.

It consisted of cars that formed a barricade from one side of the road to another.

Four men stood guard. I could see the traffic light beyond them, but it wasn't on. It was powered down.

It looked like a police officer and three good old boys. I called anyone that wore flannel, jeans, and a hat in the middle of hot weather a 'good old boy.' They didn't hold rifles, they held cross bows.

They got the memo about sound.

At least that was what I thought.

The one man made his way over. Not the law officer. He wore a Cincinnati ball cap and, holding the cross bow, walked over to the car.

"Remember," I said softly. "Act as if you are just as vulnerable."

His long sleeves were rolled up to the mid forearm and as he drew closer I saw the sores.

He barely spoke above a whisper but his face said more than any words. "Shut it off."

I didn't need to be a rocket scientist to know what he meant. I shut off the car.

Slowly, finger on the trigger of the crossbow he opened my door.

"Out," he told me.

"Mom," Sofie whimpered.

"It's okay." I moved cautiously and stepped out, lifting my hands.

"Where are you headed?" he asked,

I matched his tone. "Trying to get away from people. Wait this out."

"By killing yourself getting there?" he asked. "You can't drive a car. It can kill you at any second."

"I know. I just … we just wanted to run. Be safe."

"Put your hands down. Wait here," he instructed, then crept his way back to the others. They spoke for a few seconds, then the law man made his way to us.

I looked at his name tag. Officer Whirley.

He glanced in the car then to me. "Are they your kids?"

"One is. The other is a neighbor who lost her family too."

"You're insane. You can not be traveling in a car. You can't be out at all. Did you not hear the last broadcast?"

I shook my head. "Not all of it. We were scared. We just ran. Everyone was dying in our town."

"What town?"

"Carthage."

He nodded. "Well, we've known for a couple days. We implemented things right away. You can't find a safer place."

"That's good to know," I said.

"Get your things. Leave the vehicle here. It will still be here when it's over. We can give you shelter."

"We want to go to the campgrounds near the reserve."

"And you can," he said. "But you have to walk there. There is no way in hell we are letting you drive a car anywhere near our town. Once again, I'll say it. Get your things and follow me. You want to be safe? This is the place to be."

Something told me he wasn't really giving us an option. If we decided to walk the reserve and not stay, I didn't think that would be allowed.

Even though I felt as if he was placing us under some sort of unspoken arrest, I didn't feel like we were prisoners, but detainees. In the back of my mind I suspected it could happen, that's why I wanted to go around the town. They were protecting their town and we were a possible danger.

I understood that.

I got it.

We gathered our carrying items, leaving the hidden food in the car. Keys tucked in the front pocket of my jeans, the three of us followed Officer Whirley.

Again, we weren't prisoner. I was certain we could leave. I just had to figure out how.

TWENTY-NINE
INTERNMENT

Officer Whirley wasn't the one in charge. I didn't know that for sure, but I felt it as we walked with him and another man into town.

He and the others seemed more like lackies than leaders.

We carried our belongings into the small town, down the main street lined with businesses. All of them closed.

Not a soul in town, no one to be seen.

But strange flyers were put up everywhere.

A single hand drawn eye.

We turned down a street, a bank on one corner, café on the other. The street was clearly marked 'dead end.' A few houses lined the first portion, along with a closed and boarded up auto body shop.

Then after an overgrown lot to the left and old playground to the right, we entered what I knew would be our living arrangements.

The forgotten portion of town.

The street widened and formed a circle. To call it a cul-de-sac would be creating a visualization of a perfect little residential street. Instead, the neighborhood looked like it had seen better days and it smelled bad too. There was an odd scent I couldn't place.

Some of the homes were trailers, the other small modular homes.

In the center of the cul-de-sac circle was a broken flagpole and huge fire pit, or it looked like one.

Odd placement.

People sat outside in lawn chairs, some on porches. There were quite a few people. They stared at us as we walked through. Trudging along the sidewalk, following Whirley.

I had no idea where we were going. Then I saw a woman standing on the porch of a small red and white house.

We headed her way.

The woman was tall, thicker built, but not heavy. Almost as if she had been a body builder in her younger years.

Her hair was curly brown in a longer, short style and I knew the second I saw her, this was the person in charge.

Something was in her hand, rolled up paper. She gave a look as if she were trying to be pleasant but firm.

A 'hey, I'm approachable' but 'don't mess with me' look.

As we walked toward her, I didn't know if we'd arrived at her headquarters slash home; I didn't know what was going on.

But I knew that at that moment we approached, everyone went inside.

She waited until the last door softly closed.

"People generate energy," she spoke quietly. "If you're wondering why they left."

"This is Stacey," Whirley said. "She was mayor ... is mayor."

Stacey extended the paper to me. "These are our rules. Simple to follow. We enforce them. They are for your safety as much as everyone else's. You can stay here in this house." She motioned her hand back.

It was weird. It had this creepy horror movie feeling about it all.

The screen porch door was removed. Shifting my eyes, I noticed not a single home had a storm door on the front door.

"We'll need to check your bags for weapons.," she said.

"You know what?" Avon spoke up, almost chipper.

Stacey's face turned stone and red. "We speak in a whisper. What is wrong?"

"Sorry, just ..." Avon lowered her voice. "Nervous. And thank you. I'm going to walk."

"What?" I asked.

"The policeman said I could walk to the reserve. I'm gonna walk the forty miles."

"Are you nuts?" I questioned.

"Al, it's for the best." She stared at me. "Maybe you'll come around in the decision."

I watched her eyebrow raise. Was she trying to convey something to me in some sort of code? If so, I wasn't getting it.

"No," Stacey spoke firm. "You're not going anywhere."

"I'm not a prisoner," Avon replied. "I'm not under arrest."

"Nope. You are our guest," Stacey said. "I can't take a chance on those of us remaining with someone running around out there. Making noise, doing something to cause harm. Authorities say up to six weeks for us to heal. That's what we'll do. Make yourself comfortable." She stepped between us and down the stairs of the porch. "Whirley, check their bags."

I slowly slipped my bag from my shoulder and followed Stacey.

I didn't call out, I just kept up, walking briskly across the cul-de-sac until she noticed I followed and she stopped.

"You can't make us stay here," I said. "We want to go to the cabins."

"I can't take that chance," she replied. "I can't. I'm sorry. We lost so many already and some to the carelessness of strangers passing through. Follow the rules. It won't be long. It's for your protection as well. You'll thank me when you're still alive."

They couldn't enforce it. There was no way.

If they worried about sound and energy, they would do very little to stop us.

We'd leave.

There was an arrogance about her that rubbed me the wrong way. A power trip. One she probably was waiting on her whole life. Now she had it, the ability to control everything.

Not me.

Not my daughter.

Not Avon.

I'd play her game until I could figure out how to slip from under her nose.

They were being ridiculous if they thought they could keep us in their crappy town just by telling us we had to stay. We left Carthage because I didn't want to be around death, I wasn't staying in another town to watch it die.

Thank her? Really? Please.

I'd keep myself and my daughter alive. I didn't need her or that town.

Then as I crossed the cul-de-sac a chill went up my spine.

I paused at the firepit and flagpole and realized, upon first glance, they weren't what I thought.

There was something beyond demanding about the people in the town.

They were brutal.

It wasn't a holiday gathering spot, a 'look to the flag and sing by a fire' kind of place. It was something ominous.

What I thought had been a flagpole, wasn't. It was a post, possibly part of an old basketball hoop. And it wasn't charcoal or burnt wood that created the ashes. It was human remains. I knew that right away when I saw the partial hand on the outskirts of the fire base.

Was it some sort of sacrificial pit? I didn't know what they were up to, nor did I want to find out.

I just knew we were getting out of there and fast.

How hard would it be?

THIRTY
RULES OF SILENCE

Day Eight

We should have backed up. When we saw them, Whirley and the others, standing there as a human roadblock, we … I … should have known better.

Back up the SUV and go.

Turn around.

Find another way.

We didn't. I wasn't thinking, I truly wasn't. In my mind they formed a roadblock to protect their town, let no one through. Instead, they were in the mindset they wanted no danger close.

Anyone that could make a noise was a threat.

Keep them close, under watch … keep them silent.

The town of Silver Bend was probably a small gem before everything went sideways.

A perfect two block main street lined with businesses and a grocery store that made our little market look like a Super Walmart.

I had heard of the town but never had been there.

Eight side streets led to the residential areas with a few homes scattered around the town in the country.

We found out a lot from Whirley as he checked our bags and took our only two weapons.

The day of the flash they had a community event. Seventy-five percent of the town was out in the community park.

All outside.

All exposed.

On that fateful afternoon on Memorial Day there were six hundred and eighty-four people in Silver Bend.

Now they were a few shy of a hundred.

Twenty percent of us were strangers, passing by, trying to get around. Trapped now in a concrete 'children of the corn' world.

Unlike in Carthage, the bulk of those who died in Silver Bend ignited two days after the flash.

They weren't scattered deaths. A huge portion of their town died nearly at once.

It prompted Mayor Stacey into overdrive to seek answers. What happened? Why did her town suddenly burn to ashes?

She didn't say how she got her answers, she didn't say much. Whirley said they knew a few days before we arrived and immediately snapped into protective survival mode.

Rules of engagement or rather rules of silence were listed on the piece of paper left for us at the house.

Staying in that house was like stepping back in time. A two-bedroom, one-story, red-and-white siding home complete with Jalousie windows in the kitchen and bathroom. A painted iron railing surrounded the four-by-four slab concrete porch. The kitchen cabinets were decades old and the Formica countertop hadn't been updated probably since the house was built.

It was clean.

It wasn't run down.

We spent the night totally expecting to leave the next day. To slip out, unnoticed, not followed.

Sofie pointed out that with such detailed rules, the people in Silver Bend weren't taking chances.

The moment one of us stepped outside, whether it was the front door or the back, someone was there watching.

I didn't know if it was just our street or all over town, but there were watch guards. Armed with cross bows and tasers.

The idea of jolting someone into flames wasn't just exclusive to us, I guessed.

The rules sheet told us if we needed anything where we were to go, when and how.

The rule sheets. It was obvious they'd developed a plan, sat down and wrote down every single rule. The sheet read ...

In order to live there must be strict guidelines.

No exceptions.

Silence is the only way.

No louder than a whisper.

No noises of any kind.

If you cannot be silent, your silence will be assured.

No cars, no vehicles of any kind.

No music, no electricity, or use of cell phones.

No shoes while in public.

If insubordination causes the loss of a life, then your life will be taken.

Eye for an eye.

Enforcers are on duty.

This is the way of life in order to preserve life.

When I read the 'eye for an eye' part, I knew exactly what they meant. Cause a person to ignite, you will be ignited. No one needed to tell me that.

The proof was in the sacrificial, Salem Witch trial style pit in the middle of the cul-de-sac.

Staring out the kitchen window, I heard the splashing of water in a container. I turned and looked over my shoulder. Sofie was shaking a near empty jug.

"We left too much water in the car, Mom," she said.

"Whirley said we could get what we need. I'll go look for drinking water," I replied.

Avon peeked out from behind me. "I wonder what would happen if we just left."

I shook my head.

"Our best defense," she said, "is the fact we can make noise and not die. We could be loud."

"They have crossbows," I told her. "You want to take a chance one of them won't aim for you."

"We can't stay here," she said. "Look at those rules."

"I know. And we'll get out. I'll go find water." I grabbed the jug. "Maybe get ideas on getting out."

"I'll go with you," Sofie said.

"No. Stay put with Avon. Maybe go outside," I suggested. "Look around. See if the watchdogs have a pattern. Something that they do which gives us an out."

"Al," Avon called my name. "I think we are worrying about this too much. We just leave. There'll be an opening."

"Did you see those rules?" I asked. "They're desperate to keep order and quiet. Desperate people do desperate things. I just have a sickening feeling about all this."

"I'm not worried about what they'll do to me," Avon said.

"And I am not worried about what they'll do to me, either," I replied. "I'm worried about what they might do to my child. I'll be back."

With the nearly empty jug in my hand, I kissed my daughter and ventured out. I didn't have any idea what I would face, but I had to see what was out there. What we were up against.

Hopefully the town wasn't as bad as that rule sheet made it out to be.

THIRTY-ONE
BEAKS DON'T LIE

I wasn't in the right mindset. More than likely, I probably hadn't been in the right mindset since everything started. For a fact, I hadn't processed anything, nor had I grieved properly. I was too worried about my child. I'd wanted to protect her but I had put her in a more dangerous situation.

We didn't know anyone.

Maybe leaving Carthage wasn't the best idea. I couldn't take the death, yet there we were in another town. Although their rules of silence made it seem as if I wouldn't see death as much.

Still, I just wanted to be away from everything.

While I wasn't in danger of igniting, nor was my daughter, we were in danger of accidently causing someone else to ignite.

Leaving and hiding out was the responsible thing to do. Not to mention I wasn't sure how people would treat us knowing we didn't have the same risk as they did.

For that first day I had to pull a scouting mission, find out what we were truly up against. Maybe they weren't all that bad and they had everyone's best interest in mind. Maybe I thought the worst because it wasn't what I wanted.

With that empty plastic milk gallon jug in my hand, I walked down the street toward the main road of town.

I passed the first guard that stood in the cul-de-sac, he watched me for a second, but didn't say anything. Then when I neared the main street another guard with a crossbow was there. He stopped me, no words came from his mouth, he just pointed to my feet.

I was confused and shook my head showing him so.

With the end of the cross bow, he tapped my shoe and mouthed the word "off."

My shoes.

That was right.

It was in the rules. I thought maybe it had to do with static in the house. But it had more to do with noise. In fact, the street was so quiet I did hear my own footsteps.

I lifted a hand apologetically and immediately removed my boots. I placed them on the sidewalk near a front yard and whispered, "I'll be back for them."

He nodded and I showed him the jug.

He pointed to the right.

I acknowledged what he did with a grateful look and headed in the direction I was given.

I hated walking without shoes. I moved slowly. Clearly there were ash remnants on the ground, and I tiptoed a lot.

It wasn't just humans, it was animals.

Birds especially, so many. They didn't ignite like humans. Their feet and beaks remained. Like shells washing up to the beach, the beaks were everywhere.

There were people walking, much like me. Silently creeping. I had never in my life heard it so quiet there was a buzz in my ear. A half block down the street, just outside the food market, a line formed in the street. It was only about four people deep and I could see they stood by a water buffalo.

One man stood by it distributing the water.

He was younger and even from where I stood, he didn't look well.

In line, as if some sort of car alarm, the sound of a stomach gurgling rang out startling everyone.

People jumped back looking for the culprit.

It caused a pause, then water distribution continued.

It took a long time. How many jugs were people filling?

It certainly wasn't the woman in front of me. I knew for a fact she only held one jug.

When hers was filled, it seemed to take every bit of her strength to carry it. She embraced it like a baby in her arms.

When it was my turn, I looked at the young man. It wasn't my imagination. He wasn't well. He was gaunt, his face almost white, it was so pale. He had burns on his hand, but I thought the culprit was his neck wound. A small slice right under his Adams apple that was red and inflamed, obviously infected.

I felt bad for him.

He was sick, working, and by the depth of his burns wasn't far from igniting. Surely, just locking himself away in silence would slow the effects in his body.

However, he was made to man the water.

I handed him my jug. The timid young man was frightened, I could tell. Seeing the way he acted, the way he filled the jugs, I knew why it was taking so long.

No more than a trickle came from the water buffalo. That was on purpose. A stream slow enough not to make a noise.

When my jug was finally full, I thanked him and turned.

Suddenly, I became conscious of every noise I made. Every splash of the water, the gentle tap of my bare feet on the street.

I was scared to cause any disturbance. I felt as if every person in Silver Bend was that little guy in the game 'Don't Break the Ice' and that any move I made could be their last. But instead of falling through the broken simulated ice, they'd burst into flames.

I walked thirty feet behind the frail older women from in front of me in the water line. She didn't walk far before a woman, younger and looked about seven or eight months pregnant, came and carried the water for her.

I thought they were mother and daughter, the way they walked and moved. There was even a resemblance, but that could have been my imagination. If I wasn't mistaken, I recognized the pregnant woman from our street. When I had seen her it made me shudder. Simply because not only was it her that was vulnerable but her unborn child.

The duo moved in the same direction as I did, then suddenly it happened.

The older woman stepped on something, the loud scream came from her before I watched her buckle over.

I had heard screams and under normal circumstances it would have been attention getting but this time, it sent people running. They flew in every direction and ducked inside. Even I felt the shock of the broken silence. It caused my heart to jump.

I raced over to her. The younger woman was trying to help the older woman as she sat on the ground. It was only a single scream, but the damage was done.

It jumped started my heart like an AED and I supposed it happened to a lot. But the human body in the post flash state was frail and vulnerable.

I arrived at the woman, she stifled her cries while holding her bloody foot. A beak had impaled her.

I heard the daughter whisper a horrified, "No" and her eyes widened.

Without needing to see, I smelt what was happening.

Looking over my shoulder I saw someone fully engulfed in flames. I didn't know if it was a man or woman, but I knew what caused the sudden ignition.

And it would happen again if something wasn't done, because upon seeing what her scream of pain had caused, the older water jug woman screamed again.

Instinctively, my hand shot straight to her mouth in an attempt to silence her.

"Shh. Shh," I begged her, keeping my hand over her mouth, close to suffocating her.

Quickly her wide eyes shifted back and forth, tears welled in them, and flowed over my hand. It didn't take long for someone to come.

Two men, saying nothing, pushed me out of the way, sending me back to the concrete.

The rule sheet mentioned enforcers and I guessed the two men were part of that team. The way they acted, moved and were aggressive, it was easy to tell they were given a position of some sort of power.

One of them had a cross bow and they each took hold of one of her arms and yanked her to her feet.

I knew it was coming again.

The beak was still in the sole of her foot and the moment they made her stand, she screamed again as it jammed farther into her skin.

I understood how painful it was, but why did she keep screaming? Even if it wasn't against those stupid rules, she had to know she was putting others in danger. Perhaps her own child if the pregnant girl was her child.

She screamed and screamed and then …

Silence.

They didn't kill her.

Quickly one of them plunged something into the base of her throat. He retracted his hand and blood poured out from the small puncture wound.

They released their grip of her and her hands shot to her throat.

She tried to scream again, but she only gurgled as blood came from her mouth as well.

Both men stepped back. I was near them. I wanted to stop them. They were delivering justice right there on the street.

Were they serious?

I saw the one lift the orange taser and aim.

He whispered, "By order of Mayor Stacey Gallagher, for the death of Jason Wilkens, you are sentenced to immediate death."

Then the daughter, doing what any daughter would do, bellowed.

She cried out, "Mom! No!"

They didn't need to shoot. The jug woman looked at her daughter and in a second her abdomen glowed bright orange and the inevitable ignition occurred.

Jug woman couldn't scream but I saw her mouth open as she tried.

Flames encompassed her and her street cremated body toppled to the ground.

The enforcer with the taser aimed at the daughter and the other man stopped him.

"No." He shook his head. "She did our job. We just take her to the bank."

The bank?

I didn't know what that meant until they grabbed the daughter and escorted her down the street.

Her shoulder bounced in her weeping as she walked.

That fast.

It was done.

I stood two feet from the ash remains of Jug woman. Part of her arm remained, along with a belt buckle. I could even see that beak.

It survived again.

I also realized why they didn't kill the daughter sight unseen like they had with the mom.

Justice delivered.

Jug woman's scream caused a death, and the daughter's scream sealed her mother's fate.

It was, without a doubt, eye for an eye.

THIRTY-TWO
ESCAPE

Where was she?

My mind spun with anger.

I screamed out, "where was this so-called mayor of Silver Bend."

I asked, no one answered me.

The only people that actually replied were the enforcers and they're response was, "Go back to your house."

"I want to speak to her."

"Keep asking," one said to me. "You won't ask again."

"Wait. Are you threatening me?" I asked in a whisper.

"No, just please stop talking."

There was something about the way he said it. A certain plea to his tone that was sincere.

I nodded, and with my water headed back to the house. But I wasn't stopping.

"Make sure everything is together," I told Sofie. "We're leaving."

"They said we can go?" she asked.

"They shouldn't be holding us," I replied.

Avon stepped closer. "Are we just going to walk out? Go?"

"Yeah."

"Mom." Sofie shook her head. "That's not a good idea. I really think that's a bad idea. People are scared. Nobody talks. I mean it goes beyond afraid of catching fire." She dropped her voice. "Did you see the burning post out there?" She pointed.

"I did."

Avon asked, "Why are they burning people or are they putting them there because they're about to ignite? You know, maybe stop them from doing damage."

"They're making them ignite. It's that eye for an eye rule. It's insane." I walked to the door.

"Where are you going?" Sofie asked.

"To find this Stacey person. I'll try telling her we're leaving. I'll tell her nicely."

"And if she says we can't?" Sofie asked.

"I'll kill her."

"Mom!"

I cringed. "No, I won't kill her. That just slipped out. I'll just let her think we're being complacent. Then we'll leave. They're all scared. Even the enforcers. They'll only go so far and do so much. I haven't seen one yet not marked, so they stand a chance of igniting as well. Don't worry …" I opened the door. "I'll find her and we'll leave. Simple as that."

"You can't leave," Stacey said bluntly. "It's as simple as that."

I'd found her.

Quietly and barefooted, I searched that entire town and then I recalled them saying they were taking the younger woman to 'the bank.' I thought it was a code word of sort until I saw Stacey leaving actually a bank.

She wouldn't stop, so I followed.

Finally, about a block and a half away, she spun on her heals huffed at me and pointed back to the way we just came.

"What?" I mouthed the words.

She stormed to me with a low voice. "You obviously need to talk, why else would you be stalking me?"

"I do."

"Then head back to the bank," she instructed.

I would be a fool if I wasn't a little apprehensive about that. After all, I watched them drag a woman to the bank and made it seem like punishment.

I kept my distance, making sure none of her goons followed us.

When we walked inside the old bank, a gray-haired gentleman wearing scrubs stepped from what clearly was the vault.

He glanced at Stacy with shock.

"No," she said. "We're here to talk."

She waved for me to follow. I couldn't help but try to see inside the vault that the medical person stood by guardingly.

Slowing down my pace, I could see a long table and a pair of legs.

Stacey cleared her throat and held the door to a backroom open.

The walls of the room had dark tinted glass and she closed the door the second I stepped inside.

She spoke normally. "Talk."

"Oh, no whisper?"

"Clearly, you weren't affected. Neither was I."

"Then why did we have to come in here?" I asked.

"Because I care about those who are vulnerable. What … do … you … want?"

"This is all a bit much just for me to tell you I am leaving. Rather we are leaving."

Stacey folded her arms and chuckled. "You're leaving."

"Yes. We're leaving. It's as simple as that."

"You can't leave," she said bluntly. "It's as simple as that."

"We're not your prisoners."

"No, you're not. You're a risk."

"What?" I laughed.

"You're a risk. Because you aren't affected, and you just don't have that worry."

"We leave, you don't have to worry," I said.

"Where are you going?" she asked.

"To the reserve."

"To get there, you have to go around our town and hit Samsonville or you go through and hit Barkley."

"The highway."

210

"Barkley again. It's at the interchange," she said. "I can't take a chance of you driving anywhere. Making a noise that can get someone killed. Right now, believe it or not you're a potential murderer, we all are."

"We'll walk."

"Really. Sixty miles? You might as well stay put. It will take you nearly as long to get there as to wait out the danger. Danger to others. Wait here, then head home or wherever."

"We don't want to."

"I don't understand why not."

"Because you're insane. You're a mad woman."

Stacey laughed at me. "How do you figure?"

"I just watched your … enforcers sentence a woman to death on the street. That post in the middle of the street, there are remains there."

"An eye for an eye. You tell me what to do. I'm up for suggestion. What is your solution?"

"Not immediately kill them."

"So you suggest no punishment," she stated. "People can make whatever noise they want and if it results in someone's death, it's okay for them to say, 'my bad, I didn't mean it?'" She shook her head. "There has to be consequences for not being quiet, especially when it costs a life."

I didn't have a response nor a reasonable suggestion. I was placed on the spot.

"You come in here and you don't even know, do you?" she asked. "Any noise can set it off. Any ... especially if the marks have extended higher than the elbow. Anywhere above the waist. A spark, static noise from a radio, a snap of a fucking finger. I know, I've seen it. I'm tired of seeing it."

"I am too, that is why I want to go. That ..." I said passionately, "is why I left home in the first place."

"And if people sit back, be quiet, it will be over within six weeks. That's what scientists in the UK have told us."

"You can't force people not to make a sound. Even if it's in their best interest."

"Then we make them quiet."

"What does that even mean?" I asked.

"It means if you can't be quiet then we make you quiet."

I was totally confused and then it hit me. The people on my street didn't talk, the young man in the water line. He didn't speak, he had a fresh scar on his neck. The doctor ... the bank ...

They were performing surgery to silence people.

"You're quieting them," I said in disgust. "You're making it so they can't talk."

"If they can't follow the rules. We ensure it by any means necessary."

"You're insane. And we're out of here ... by any means necessary."

"And we'll stop you."

"Wanna say by any means necessary? Don't bother." Wanting to just blast her, I refrained, instead I stormed out as fast as I could in my bare feet.

<><><><>

The water jug woman's pregnant daughter was back on our street. I saw her when I retrieved my shoes still setting where I left them.

She sat slanted on a porch chair, a bandage around her neck. She looked at me as I walked by, perking up slightly.

I walked toward her porch and mouthed the words, "I'm sorry." And headed back to the house where we had been staying.

As I made it to the house, I noticed everyone was outside. Silent, scared looks upon their faces. They looked as if they were scared of me.

Had they been silenced for noise insubordination? Before going into the house, I walked around the back to the yard. I wanted to see where it went. Was it a viable escape route?

A thick patch of trees blocked my view. If we could get far enough ahead, we could make it back to the highway and to our car.

I was certain it was still there.

They wouldn't touch it.

Hurriedly, I made my way back into house and closed the door.

I glanced to the feet of my daughter and new friend, they had their shoes on.

I felt better about that.

"I'm getting my shoes on," I said to Sofie and Avon. "Get your shit. We're leaving."

"Did you figure out how?" Sofie asked.

"Yeah, we leave out the back. Run through the woods and get to the car. We just need to get far enough away."

"Thank God," Avon replied. "My bag is already packed."

"Mine's by the door," said Sofie.

"Mine's ready, too," I added.

"What made you finally decide?" Avon asked.

"I watched a woman get sentenced to death on the street and her daughter dragged off and vocal cords cut. At least I think that's what they did. They silenced her. That's what they do when you make noise. She has a bandage on her throat."

"Oh my God," Avon gasped.

"Yeah, you can see her. The pregnant woman. First house on the right," I said. "Just sitting on the porch."

Sofie walked over and grabbed her bag. She looked out the window. "Mom, we might have trouble."

I walked to the window and peered out. Stacey was walking toward our house, two of her crossbow armed enforcers with her.

"Mom, what did you do?"

"Nothing." I lifted Sofie's bag and handed it to her. "Let's go now."

"Out the back?" Avon asked.

"Yes."

The three of us moved quickly. I grabbed my bag in my run and we raced out the back door as quiet as we could, off the porch and straight across the yard toward the woods.

We didn't run together, just in the same direction. Sofie was ahead of me, I knew that. I looked back once to check on Avon, she kept up close.

I didn't see anyone else. No enforcers, no Stacey.

We were in the clear.

We had to be.

A good distance into the trees, I was confident we could slow down. They let us go.

That was my thinking.

I didn't even think twice about the slight air like whistle or the snap of twigs until I heard the grunt.

My feet came to a stop, I looked back to see Avon on the ground. She rolled over and her neck stretched and back arched. I could see the arrow in her thigh and she withered and fidgeted in pain.

I ran back to her, sliding down to the ground. The arrow had gone into the side of her thigh, through the fleshy part.

How she wasn't screaming was beyond me.

"Go," she whispered.

"No. Get up." I reached down for her.

"Go." Her hand sloppily laid on mind and she dropped a set of keys.

I clutched them in my hand, then placed them in my back pocket as I peered over my shoulder to check on Sofie.

She had stopped.

I waved for her to go and she shook her head, walking back.

What the hell are you doing? I thought. *Go. Go. Go.*

Returning my views to Avon, I saw them approach. Stacey and her enforcers.

One aimed at me, the other at my daughter.

"When danger is over," Stacey said quietly, "you can go. Until then, you stay." She glanced down to Avon. "By any means necessary."

<><><><>

The pregnant girl's name was Julie. At least that was what Dr. Mason called her when he came to our house to tend to Avon.

The enforcers carried her back and Stacey was smug about it. She had this shit eating grin when she said, "Looks like you're going nowhere." She left with her thugs once the doctor arrived.

I didn't get it. Why were we treated like such a threat? Why would they hurt Avon?

More than anything I wanted to pummel her, but that wasn't happening. I had to worry about Avon and my daughter.

Julie had come over not long after Stacey left.

She stood on our porch, lingering there, peeking in, waiting for an invite.

Sofie saw her out there and that was when Dr. Mason said who she was.

He then got right to work. He pulled the arrow out of Avon's thigh right in the middle of the living room. He had sedated her first, knocked her out and she didn't make a noise.

He worked on her leg like it was second nature, probably moved just as quickly and efficiently with the vocal cord procedure as well.

People did things fast when they did them all the time.

One thing I did notice when he operated, he didn't have any marks. Like Stacey he wasn't affected.

Sofie stood behind the couch watching and I decided to go outside in case there was something Julie needed.

The moment I walked out to the porch, she weakly grabbed my hands and looked at me as if to convey some sort of gratefulness.

There was fear in her wide eyes.

I once saw the old movie *Planet of the Apes* and she reminded me of the woman, Nova, that didn't speak.

"I'm sorry about your mom," I told her.

She nodded and looked at the window.

"She'll be fine. I think. You need to sit. You look …" I glanced down to her hands and I didn't see any marks. "Wait." I hurriedly and visually examined her. "You have no burns."

She shook her head.

That made me smile. "Baby is okay then."

She nodded, then her head quickly lifted.

I glanced over my shoulder. Sofie stood there.

My daughter waved for me to come inside.

I did and invited Julie to come in as well.

217

Julie closed the door.

Dr. Mason walked to me and handed me a pill bottle. "These are her antibiotics. She needs to be on these ten days. Three times a day. The arrows aren't sterile. If she doesn't get an infection, she should be fine in a week. She shouldn't walk for a couple days."

"When can we run?" I asked.

"You really want to try that again."

"I don't get it," I said. "I don't. We leave on foot. What is the big deal?"

"You're out there. You're a threat."

I had never met anyone I had instant contempt for, but I did for him and it fueled an anger when he glanced at Julie.

"Don't look at her. How can you even look at her knowing what you did," I said.

Julie reached out, touching my arm as if to silence me.

"I did what needed to be done."

"How can you, as a medical professional, be so complacent in these inhumane rules? I mean Stacey says cut the vocal cords and you say where."

"Actually, the laryngectomy was my idea. Considering, from what I have seen, the human voice is a huge trigger. A scream can instantly cause several people to incinerate."

"You're a monster," I told him.

He shook his head. "You can't judge me. I am doing what I can to keep people alive. To make it through the healing process. To make sure no one has to burn. To make sure my daughter doesn't burn. Your child is fine, there's no fear of her burning yet you're running to what? Keep her safe? I will go to any extreme to keep my child safe, any. I suspect … so would you. Find me if you need me for your friend." He nodded at Julie and then left.

His words seared into me.

He would go to any extreme and he was right, I would go to any extreme as well.

I already had and would go farther.

We all would.

That was what was happening. In our own selfish best interest, we were doing what it took.

I wondered if after the healing occurred could we as a human race even come back from all the horrific things that we did?

I doubted that we could.

THIRTY-THREE
UNEXPECTED

Day Seventeen

I never thought I would see the day when I'd witness what happened to the human body as it slowly cooked from the inside out for two weeks.

The skin was dark, blistered, I couldn't believe some of them were still alive.

There were still weeks of silence left until the 'supposed' healing time had passed. Stacey and Dr. Silencer said they had seen people getting better. I hadn't.

At least not on our street.

Things grew worse if that was even possible.

They added to the rules about food distribution. They rationed everything.

No longer could we go get water everyday or even food, we had to wait.

I wanted people to revolt against Stacey and her rules, but they didn't. They stayed silent and complacent.

I wanted to leave but Avon was in no condition to try another escape and I wasn't leaving her behind.

So we stayed and weathered through her infection. It was a hot mess and I worried that it was going to get so bad, they'd want to cut it off.

However, ten days after being hit by that arrow, Avon was feeling motivated especially after the events of the night before.

A week and a half earlier I met a young man named Charlie at the water buffalo. My daughter ended up befriending him. The silent young man conveyed how he had lost his entire family and, by the looks of him, he didn't have long. Then again, I'd thought that when I saw him that first time. We'd taken him in, and for a short time he was one of our little group.

He was a good kid.

Was.

He made the stupid mistake of sneaking into the kitchen of a home near the water buffalo, frightened the owner when she saw him taking a can of soup and she ignited.

That night in some sort of demented ritual, Stacey and her goons tied Charlie to a post in the cul-de-sac and played music until he burst into flames.

A display for all to see.

Twisted and sick. It mortified my daughter and all I could do was hold her in my clutches, covering her mouth, and wait for it to be over.

I wanted out of Silver Bend and with Avon healing, we would try again.

Sofie sat by the window staring out, looking at the burning post in the middle of the street.

"Soon, we'll be out of here," I told her.

"What's the use, Mom?"

"What's the use? You're looking out the window where your new friend was murdered and I don't want you to have to see anyone die again. I mean it. Not violently, not like this." I kissed her on the top of the head. "I'll be back."

"Where are you going?"

"To check on Julie."

I worried about the young woman. Alone, scared, and pregnant, I wanted to take her and the baby under my wing. Get her out of town before that baby came. She had another month, but she had been having Braxton hicks for a couple days.

With all the stress, anything was possible. At the very least, I thought maybe she should move into the house with Sofie, Avon, and me.

I left the house, quietly of course, but I paused as I passed the burning post.

Glancing down to the ashes, I looked. Searching for something. Usually some body part remained, something to bury. A foot, ear, hand … something. But nothing remained of Charlie.

My mind kept thinking he was in a better place, then again, any place was better than Silver Bend.

When I arrived at Julie's small walkway, I could see Stacey and Dr. 'Silencer' Mason through her window. I quickly picked up the pace and in some sort of protective way, I walked right into her house.

Julie sat on the couch, staring down to her hands while Stacey and the doctor stood above her.

"What's going on?" I asked. "Everything okay? Julie? Is everything okay?"

"Isn't that nice of you to take a special mother role with her," Stacey said snidely. "We were just checking on her, making sure she knew to come to the bank when labor begins."

I laughed at that. "Really? Why? She won't make a sound, you cut out her vocal cords."

Doctor Mason replied, "It's not for her, it's for the baby."

"Babies cry," I said. "What are you gonna do? Keep the baby in the vault until the healing is done."

"Don't be ridiculous," Stacey again, spoke snidely.

"Okay so why have the baby born in the vault, he isn't only gonna cry when he's born, he'll ..." I paused when it hit me what they were going to do. "Are you kidding me?"

Stacey stepped close to me. "Lower your voice."

"Babies cry."

"And crying babies can cause ignition, we know this."

"Are you gonna do an eye for an eye on the baby?"

"No. If the baby is born after everyone is healed, no worries. If he's early, we'll make sure it doesn't get to that point."

When she turned to walk away, I grabbed her arm.

"Get your hand off of me," she growled her voice.

I lifted my hand from her. "I fucking hate you," I whispered hard.

"Who cares?"

"Oh, I do. When this is all said and done, I'm coming back for you. That I promise."

She stared with a serious expression then her lips twitched and puckered and she softly snorted the laugh she tried to stifle. She didn't take me seriously, not at all.

"If you'll excuse me, I have to walk away from your threats," she said. "We have a newcomer arriving."

Doctor Mason stood by the front door looking out. "Team's back."

"And here they are. Have to tell the rules." She stepped outside.

Exhaling, I faced Julie. "We're getting you out of here. Just let me think of how. Okay?"

Julie nodded.

"I'll be back." I walked to the front door and stepped out on to the porch.

Stacey and Doctor Mason walked toward the team. I couldn't see who they escorted. Was it one person? Two?

But as soon as they moved farther away, I saw the new arrival and my heart dropped to my stomach.

I was happy, relieved, and had a renewed sense of energy.

It wasn't a rescue and I didn't look at it as such. It was another number on our side.

The airy words of, "Oh my God," came from my mouth and with a huge grin and arrogant attitude, I stepped off that porch.

Cody had arrived.

THIRTY-FOUR
VAIN RESCUE

Cody didn't see me. Not at first. He looked confused, irritated, and maybe even angry. Much like I imagine I looked when we arrived.

I couldn't figure out why he was there. He was either looking for us or headed to the reserve himself.

There truly was no reason for him to be there. They weren't expecting him, none of the enforcers were bringing him to our street.

I watched the expression on his face. He was ready to argue, demand his freedom. I could see it, feel it, but I knew what would happen if he spoke louder than a whisper.

Hurriedly I made my way to him and caught his attention before he said anything.

Then Cody saw me.

He was confused, I saw his lips move to speak and I raced to him embracing him.

"Al, what …"

"Shh," I whispered in his ear. "Don't speak."

"What's going on?" he asked as he stepped back from the embrace.

He was probably confused why I even hugged him.

"My name is Stacey," she spoke up. "You were …"

"Stop." I held my hand up to her. "He's my friend, he'll stay with us. I'll tell him. Go away."

"What the hell?" Cody asked. He was probably shocked by my abrasiveness. "Al, what the hell?"

"Pretty much so," I said. "Welcome to your nightmare."

"My … my nightmare?" Cody asked confused.

"Your nightmare."

<><><><>

I wouldn't let Stacey say anything to him. She tried. I interrupted, pulling Cody with me to the little house.

"You can't speak," I told him. "Not above a whisper."

"At all times?"

"Yes." I felt his confusion and knew I would be able to explain more once we were out of earshot of Stacey. In a quiet world sound traveled.

We stepped inside and I closed the door. "Sofie, keep an eye on the window."

My daughter hesitated before acknowledging my request. Her eyes transfixed in surprise on Cody. "Doctor Dogan?"

"Cody?" Avon asked. "What are you doing here?"

I shut the door. "That's what I want to know. Why are you here?"

"Not expecting to find you," Cody replied. "I thought you were headed to the reserve."

"We were," I answered. "Then we got stuck in this hell loop."

"You think you're overreacting?" Cody questioned.

"Nope." I walked to the cabinet in the corner of the living room, grabbed a bottle and poured him a drink.

"It's still early in the day," he said.

"Doesn't matter. Not even drinking makes this place tolerable. Were you looking for us or just headed to the reserve?"

"I was looking for you," he said. "Craig wanted me to find you. He was worried. Just thought you'd be better at home. We lost most of our people. Some are healing now. So I came to look for you. I saw their roadblock and was gonna turn around."

"Why didn't you?" I asked.

"I saw Avon's SUV. That's when I figured you might be here."

"We are. This place is some sort of crazy nightmare world working under the guise of keeping people alive. They got us," I told him. "Now they have you."

Cody scoffed. "No, they don't. We leave."

"We can't leave, Cody. I mean we can, we will, but it won't be easy. Look at Avon's leg. They shot her with an arrow when we tried to leave."

"What?" he asked shocked. "Why?"

"Anyone out there making noise is a threat," I explained. "In here, they keep you quiet. If they have you, you aren't a threat."

There was a look of disbelief on his face.

"What?" I asked. "Why are you giving me that look?"

"It's just ... you can see why they are enforcing it right?" he stated. "I mean, not that it's right, but they're trying to save as many people as they can. This woman ... Stacey ... is she the one keeping us?"

"Enforcing it, yes." I nodded.

"Then we go talk to her," Cody said. "I'll tell her I'm a doctor and I'm needed back in our town."

"Won't work," I said.

"We can try."

Sofie looked out the window. "She's coming."

I gave a smug smile. "Now's your chance."

Stacey listened to Cody with a sympathetic look. For a second I thought I was going to be proven wrong. She truly appeared taken with the young medical examiner, listening attentively, nodding her head. For a moment I believed she would say, "Go. Yes, you made a valid argument. Please. Go."

Instead, I was right. She simply said, "I'm sorry. I can't take a chance. We're only a few days out, maybe a week, until enough of my people are healing. You understand."

He didn't.

Cody was baffled. His naivete led him to believe that all he had to do was explain his situation and Stacey would just say go.

I mean, really. Who would think we would be prisoners in a small town? But we were.

"Does she realize," Cody said, "that things are only different right now? Now ... they won't be once aid arrives and it will. The countries on the dark side of the world when the flash happened, they know. They'll be here. They're waiting. They're coming once it is safe to do so."

"Are we sure?" I asked.

Cody nodded. "And boy is she in trouble. Don't think I won't report this to someone."

With a bit of shock, I spun a look his way. "What? What are you talking about?"

"She's acting like she's Auntie Entity from *Mad Max Thunderdome*," he said. "Ever see that old movie? I did. She's acting like it. Prancing around tossing out new laws. There are procedures for that. Won't she be in for a rude awakening when she realizes this isn't the apocalypse and she is in clear violation of the Geneva Convention charter, article six paragraph C. Crimes against humanity and not the card game?"

I stepped back an inch in surprise. "Did you seriously lump Mad Max, the Geneva Convention, and a card game all into one short rant?"

"I did."

Avon shook her head. "I'm still stuck on the fact that he actually knew which article of the Geneva Convention dealt with crimes against humanity."

"What's the Geneva Convention?" Sofie asked.

"Doesn't matter." Cody waved his hand. "Just know she's in big trouble. And even if the countries bringing aid don't bring her to justice I hope she never needs any of that corn we're growing."

I was a bit baffled at Cody's attitude and belief that somehow justice was going to prevail in a world were half the planet had suddenly perished. He needed to be more angry.

Ignoring his schoolboy optimistic comments, I faced Cody. "This is what we've been living with. A cartoon tyrant. It's insane here. We need to come up with a way to go. Our vehicles are still there. We just need to get to them. They have a sacrificial pit out there that ..." I stopped talking when our front door opened and Julie walked in.

She held on to the doorframe with one hand and her stomach with the other.

I rushed to Julie. Something was wrong. The look on her face was so desperate. She gazed at me then looked down.

I knew at that moment we had to leave and leave soon.

Not just for us or Julie but for her unborn child.

We were running out of time. Her waters had clearly broken.

THIRTY-FIVE
THE WAIT

Cody looked down to a map. "I have no idea. I mean we followed the main road and turned one time which brought us to this street. The cars are both maybe a quarter mile out of town. Not far."

"Okay." I nodded. "There are two ways out of here. From what I see on the map, out the front door …"

Avon shook her head. "Which is like impossible."

"Or out the back. But that is going to have to be sneaky. One of us goes for the car, the others distract, maybe."

"That's the only way," Cody commented. "A distraction while the escape happens. They don't have guns. They aren't going to stop the car anyway, that makes noise."

Avon added, "It's farther going the back way. I mean it took us all about ten minutes to walk here." She pointed down to the map. "Straight out the back door, through the woods and stay right of this field. Run the edge to the road, that alone is a quarter mile. And if need be duck into the field."

"That's the plan. Now ..." I looked at Cody. "If we have to hightail it, how do we do it with a newborn?"

"Bundle, hold the baby close," he replied. "And try not to bounce. Whoever carries the child."

"They're gonna come for him or her," I said, "without hesitation. If they even think she is here delivering. They want her at the bank in that vault."

Cody faced Julie. "You haven't said anything. What are your thoughts? Do you want to run after the baby is born?"

Julie nodded.

"She can't talk," I told him. "See the bandage. They cut her vocal cords. Julie ..." I turned to her. "Did anyone see you walk here holding your stomach?"

She shook her head and shrugged.

"Well, we have to walk you back."

Her eyes widened and she shook her head.

"No, listen. It's just for show, okay?" I reached out for her. "You'll stand up straight and put on a good front. I know you're in pain. You have to pretend you're not. Then once we're in the house, you'll leave out the back and make your way here through the yards."

Julie nodded.

I faced Avon. "Can you go out our back door and meet her?"

"I'll do that."

"I'll hang back. I'll get things we need and act like I stayed awhile. The only ones that will say something to Stacey are the enforcers and if they don't see you leave they'll be none the wiser. Let's do this."

Julie agreed then paused to wince in pain.

"Sofie?" I called my daughter. "Anything."

"Two enforcers," she replied.

"Good. Then let's put the show on." I took hold of Julie's arm and headed to the door. As I passed Cody I saw the shocked look on his face. "What's wrong?"

"They really cut her vocal cords."

"They did. There's your article six." After those words, I walked out with Julie.

The shoeless walk the three houses to Julie's seemed like an endless journey. She put on a brave face and tried to move without showing that she was in pain.

She was.

It was early afternoon and I just had a feeling that baby was coming before nightfall.

Maybe the night would be better. Hide our escape and get the baby out of town.

It terrified me to think what they wanted to do to that baby. All in the name of keeping him or her quiet. When they easily could just have Julie take the baby from town.

It all screamed textbook apocalypse bad guys to me.

As strange as it was, I actually saw and understood the reasoning for their desperate rules to keep things quiet. I didn't agree with how far they took them, but I understood them.

They wanted to save as many as they could in Silver Bend.

I wanted to save those I cared about.

I was just done with being a part of the silent world even unwillingly.

It was time to go.

In the bottom of Julie's living room closet was a green army duffle bag. She told me it was there and I immediately went to the room where she indicated the baby items were.

It was a nursery and it was painted green with clouds and balloons. The crib was still in the box, the mattress covered in plastic.

Numerous baby items were stacked in the room, some still had ribbons.

Julie had a baby shower. They were all gifts, I could tell.

I gathered up baby items, knowing that was what we would need. Bottles, blankets, swaddles, diapers, some sleepers.

On top of the dresser was a stuffed teddy bear. A light, tan bear with strange dark ears, a red bow tie, and wide eyes.

It didn't look brand new and that told me it meant something to Julie. I grabbed it and placed it in the bag as well.

Stepping out of the nursery I noticed the wall in the hallway.

It had photographs. All of them were in the same white frame, neatly lined on the wall to show her life.

Her husband and her. There was a picture of Julie and her mother on her wedding day and another picture that stood out to me was a family picture at a picnic.

It hit me as I looked at that wall that Julie had already lost so much.

I grabbed a few of those pictures and headed back toward the kitchen where she waited. I peered out the back door and saw Avon there.

Quietly, I opened it and handed the bag to Avon.

"I won't be long," I told Julie. "Go quickly and quietly."

With a pout, Julie nodded.

"And don't have that baby," I jokingly ordered.

She gave me a quick embrace before leaving with Avon and I stayed at that door hoping no one would see.

When they had crossed the yard, I stepped back inside and bided my time.

Admittedly I was nosey, looking around, trying to find out all I could about my silent new friend.

Pay stubs in a drawer told me she worked at the grocery store and her husband was a mechanic.

After an hour, I knew it was time to leave.

I should have looked out the window.

I didn't.

Had I done so, I wouldn't have been so surprised to see Stacey and one of her enforcers approaching the porch.

I hid my surprise and pulled the door closed. "Can I help you?" I asked.

"We're here to check on Julie," Stacey said.

"She's resting."

"We'd like to check on her. Someone said they saw her holding her stomach walking to your house."

"She did. She was," I replied. "Then she threw up. She was sick. Something she ate. I brought her home."

"I just want to check …"

"She just fell asleep. I couldn't get her off the toilet, the poor thing," I said. "Let her rest."

There was a stare down moment between us. One I wasn't sure I would win. My insides twisted in nervousness.

Then Stacey relented. She nodded. "Fine. We'll check back later."

"How about I check on her later and let you know if you're needed?"

She pursed her lips smugly. "You wouldn't."

"Probably not."

"I'll be back," she said confidently.

I waited until I knew for sure she was going to walk away before I stepped off that porch and headed back to our own prison house.

I hoped that Julie had the baby before Stacey returned. But babies didn't arrive on wished time. I wanted nothing more than to get my daughter, Julie, and the baby out of Silver Bend.

I was confident I would. I had to. Especially for my daughter.

I got my Sofie into this mess and if it was the last thing I did, I would get her out of it.

THIRTY-SIX
RAT

With a slight look of worry, Cody pulled me aside and away from the sofa where Julie was in labor.

I thought for sure something was wrong.

"What is it?" I asked.

"Coffin birth," he whispered.

"I'm sorry. What?"

"Coffin birth, that is the closest thing I have been to a woman giving birth."

"What is a coffin birth?" I asked.

"It's when the baby inside the dead mother is expelled."

I winced. "You're a doctor though. You had to have gone to medical school, right?"

"You have more experience than me."

"Me?" I asked shocked. "I had two children, my son was thirteen years ago."

Avon stepped into our conversation. "If I may. Birth is a natural thing. Women had babies in fields. I'm sure if we do nothing, it'll just come out."

"Like a coffin birth," said Cody.

"Oh, stop," I told him.

Sofie's heavy sigh carried to us. "One of you watch the window. I'll deliver the baby."

We all looked at her.

I asked, "What do you know about delivering a baby?"

"Apparently just as much as you guys. Plus we covered roadside births in health last semester."

Cody pointed at her. "She has more experience. Let her take over."

"I'll do the window." Avon rushed to take Sofie's spot.

What a pathetic group we were, all adults relying on a fifteen-year-old girl who learned how to deliver a baby on the side of the road through health class.

I felt bad for Julie. She tried to be a trooper as the pains were closer and longer. I could see she was crying out but made only a gushing air sound.

Watching her, the look on her face reminded me of the silent scream made by Charlie as he burned at the stake.

Or the woman they burned four nights earlier.

It was hard to watch.

However, I was proud of my daughter.

She was amazing and it was hard to believe she was only fifteen.

The only problem she had was cutting and clamping the cord. They taught her in health to wrap the baby with the placenta in a blanket.

Cody took care of the cord while Sofie cleaned the baby's eyes, nose and mouth. It was a boy, not as small as I expected.

Then it came, the dreaded noise that the newborn infant would make.

A cat's meow, tender and soft, but the loudest noise coming from the house.

I swaddled the baby and handed him to Julie. I looked over at the pile of belongings ready to go, the items we needed to make our move.

"I know you just gave birth," I said softly. "But we are going to have to go ahead with the plan. We need to get him out of here. It's not far."

Julie nodded.

"Okay?" I asked. "Are you sure?"

Again, Julie nodded, and slowly stood.

The baby released its first real cry.

"Shit," I cringed.

Avon announced from the window, "We have to move. We have to move now. They're coming."

"Who's doing it?" Cody asked.

"Me," I replied. "I'll do it. Avon's injured. I won't take a chance with my daughter."

"Mom, I'm younger. I'm faster." Sofie stepped to me.

"I'm older and lived a longer life. I can do this. I can. See you at the car. If all goes well, you'll beat me there," I said. "I'll make it. We know what to do, right?"

Sofie nodded. She placed the swaddled bundle in my arms. I watched until they moved to the front door and I went out the back.

During those hours of labor we had it all worked out.

I knew Stacey and her enforcers would show up. They were waiting nearby, listening for the baby's cry.

I had studied that map so much it was embedded in my mind.

They would go out the front door with the duffle bag and I would hurry out the back. It was a quarter mile to the highway, but I was shielded a good bit of the way by the woods.

Unlike when we ran before, I had a head start.

When I was younger, I had this fleeting moment in time where I was all into fitness. I would run three miles a day. I had my songs I listened to, the same songs every run. I knew by the timing of the songs how far I had to go.

I started singing those songs in my head.

I looked back every once in a while to see if anyone followed.

I didn't move fast, I was afraid of falling. Gauging by where I was in the first song, I knew I wasn't far from the field.

Just as I ended that first song, I hit the field. There I would run alongside it for a few tenths of a mile and then I'd be at the road.

I heard the voices behind me.

They were following. But they were still in the woods.

They had to see me. My arms wrapped protectively around the bundle. They were close but I focused on the end of the field and the road ahead.

I knew I could duck into the high weeds, but I truly felt I didn't need to.

I heard someone call out, "There. Get her." And I picked up the pace, I gave it all I got. I had been running over ten minutes, it seemed endless at first, now the light was at the end of the tunnel.

The road.

As I emerged from the field to the road, I smiled. Cody and Sofie were standing by a car and I saw Avon's SUV pulling away. They followed the plan. Go as soon as they arrived, don't wait for me. My daughter should have gone with them, but she didn't.

Cody had a gun. He held it out, aiming, probably waiting for me to clear so he could take his shot. I knew they were behind me.

How perfectly executed the plan was.

I just needed to make it a few more feet. A few more …

Stop.

My eyes widened.

I felt it before the whistling sound of it even registered. A searing pain, pinpointed in nature, like it only hurt in one spot. It started just below my left shoulder blade.

I was certain I stammered a few steps before I actually came to a halt.

Sofie screamed. "Mom!"

Cody fired.

Suddenly the pain radiated in my chest, my eyes cast down as I fell to my knees on that road.

The arrow protruded from my chest, the tip of it embedded into the bundle in my arms.

I freed the bundle from the arrowhead. Blood saturated the blanket.

Stacey's voice was behind me. "Well, that's one way to silence the baby."

It was strange, for a second there was no pain. A shivering laugh came from me as I turned clockwise enough to see Stacey.

Two of her enforcers were aiming at me. One was on the ground dead.

I smiled at her, releasing the bundle in my arms. The teddy bear rolled from the blanket and on to the road.

The look on Stacey's face was priceless when she saw I didn't have the baby.

It wasn't over for her. Cody fired again, taking out another enforcer, and the one remaining just took off running.

I could tell she just didn't know what to do.

We bested her.

They'd chased me as planned.

I knew the second Stacey didn't see me with the group she would assume I'd run out the back door. When she didn't see the baby, another assumption was I had him. She and others pursued me while Cody, Sofie, Avon, Julie, and the baby just walked off the front porch and directly to the car.

I felt stronger than I was, even turned again, trying to stand, but I stumbled, and Cody caught me. He inched me back down to the road. My knees hit the pavement as I sat on my feet which were tucked under my body.

"Listen," Cody said softly. "Sofie and I are gonna help you to the car."

I reached for the arrow.

"No. No, no," he sputtered fast in an assuring whisper. "It doesn't look like it hit anything vital. Okay. Don't touch it. It'll clot around it and I'll figure out how to get it out. Alright."

"It's okay, Mom."

"The baby …"

"The baby is fine. They're on their way home," Cody said.

"We won, huh?" I asked.

"Yeah. We did. We'll be in even better shape as long as this arrow stays in you until …"

I saw it on his face, heard my daughter cry out at the same time I felt the pain.

It felt worse coming out than it did when it went in.

I looked down, the arrow was gone.

"No. No. No," Cody groaned out painfully. "No."

It was like a fountain, the blood just poured from my chest.

Cody grabbed desperately for me. His hands pressing against the wound. It was useless, I knew it.

I felt the life drain from me with each passing second. I felt so weak.

"Take … care of her," I choked out.

Cody stopped. His eyes met mine.

It was all I had left in me. A request to take care of my child. Weakly, I fell into him. My forehead resting against his. The warm scared breaths from his mouth hitting against my face, my daughter's muffled cries.

I didn't even think about Stacey. She wasn't deserving of my final thoughts.

I was alright with everything that was happening, everything that had happened.

Sofie would be alright, I was certain of that.

At least for us, our group, it was over.

THIRTY-SEVEN
FROM THE OTHER SIDE

My mother died.

When she told me she was going to be the decoy, that she would run out the back door and look like she had the baby in her arms … I knew.

Whoever was the decoy was the sacrifice. When the plan was hatched, we all knew it.

The baby was placed in the open duffle bag just inside the front door so we could grab it.

We all stepped out on the porch. I didn't think it would work. But that woman Stacey fell for it.

The second she realized my mom had run through the woods, she and her guys followed her on foot.

We literally walked away. No one even bothered to watch us. It was as if the baby was the only thing that mattered, that we as a group wouldn't try to leave.

She focused on my mother.

We focused on getting to the road.

The baby cried … a lot. Yet, Stacey and her enforcers were so bent on going after Mom they never bothered to determine where the sound came from.

We made it there with relative ease, no one was around.

"Go," Cody told Avon and Julie as he retrieved a hidden gun from his car. "Take the baby and go." He made sure the gun was loaded and ready.

"We'll wait," Avon replied. "I need to know she made it."

My insides twisted and turned, my heart beat out of control. I stared in the direction I knew she'd come.

Avon and Julie got in the car, and the second my mom appeared on the road they took off. Avon must have been watching in the rearview mirror.

My whole body relaxed in relief. I thought for a second that she made it.

Then I saw them chasing her.

Through the corner of my eye, I watched Cody raise that gun. He was ready to protect my mother.

But I saw it happening before she did. I watched them aim that crossbow. She was so close to us, so close to being safe.

The rest was so much a blur.

Cody just fired off his weapon emotionally then raced to my mom. I did too.

Stacey said something, I don't know what it was. Mom heard her, because she had this semi smile as she exposed the teddy bear.

I didn't think for a single moment, standing there alone, that woman would be so bold as to deliver the final blow to my mother.

She pulled the arrow from my mother and took off.

I couldn't chase her, neither could Cody, we worried about my mother.

She was our focus.

"Al, hold on, okay, hold on," Cody told her. He held his hand firm to her chest, trying hard to stop the bleeding. "Hold on."

I was crying, screaming, lost, angry and hurt.

"Sofie, hold this." Cody lifted the bear and pressed it against my mother's wound. "Hold this tight as I lift her."

Emotionally I nodded and pressed that bear as hard as I could. Maybe if I pressed it with all of my might it would stop the bleeding.

Cody lifted her into his arms. I never stopped the pressure as he carried her to his car.

It was difficult to maneuver, opening the back door, not letting go of the bear, sliding inside at the same time he placed her in the backseat with me.

I saw the blood on his arms when he closed the door. He didn't waste a second getting in the car and driving.

In the back seat of the car, my mother was in my arms. Her head against my shoulder, cheek to my cheek. My arm wrapped around her holding that bear, but I knew it wasn't going to work. The bear was covering one wound, but she still bled from her back. I could feel it against me.

She struggled to look at me, struggled to focus.

"I'm sorry, Mommy. I'm so sorry. I love you."

"Baby … it's okay," she coughed, her fingers trying to grip my arm. "It's okay. I love …"

I watched the color drain from her, then I watched the life leave her. She went from pale to a gray, then finally this eerie, almost unrealistic white.

When her arm dropped, I knew she was gone.

It wasn't fair. She was all I had left.

My arms clenched on to her, holding my mother as tight as I could.

It was all I had left of her, those final moments in that car and I wasn't letting go.

I didn't know if I ever could.

THIRTY-EIGHT
RETURN THE FAVOR

Day Twenty-Seven

The chief and Cody wanted us back in town so badly, they fixed up the Davonsmith house on the edge of town as a place for us to stay. They knew my mother wanted to be away from the death, and they just wanted her home.

Not many survived in Carthage and they wanted us home.

We buried my mom in the backyard next to my dad and the grave we marked for my grandmother.

I lost my dad but losing my mom was different. We had been through a lifetime in a short period, we went through it together.

The world on the brink of extinction.

All she wanted to do was get away from the suffering and it led us to even more.

I didn't want to leave in the first place.

Why? Why did we even go?

It wasn't worth it.

I tried to make sense out of it all. I was so angry … so very angry.

The only good to come out of it was Julie and the baby. I kept telling myself, had it not been for my mother, the baby wouldn't be alive, maybe not even Julie.

It was the only thing I could tell myself to justify or make sense out of my mother's death.

Even though Avon's house was fine, she stayed with me, Julie, and the baby in the Davonsmith house.

It had been ten days since our return. Carthage was quiet just like Silver Bend, but there wasn't anyone to enforce the rules.

Cody said less people were dying and daily he was seeing signs of improvement in those affected.

It was almost over.

But really for me it wasn't.

Not yet.

A part of me wasn't settled, neither was Avon. We knew there was something we had to do.

A lot of things probably tipped off Cody about what we were going to do. Maybe it was gut instinct, or the map on the table when he came to check on the baby.

Or even the fact that Avon and I looked as if we were ready to walk out the door.

We were.

He didn't address it at first, in fact he rambled, trying to distract us.

251

"So, we made radio contact," Cody said. "The first of the rescue teams arrived in the US three days ago."

"Okay," Avon said dismissively.

"You know what this means, right?" Cody asked. "Help is on the way."

"Help?" Avon asked. "What kind of help? We made it through the worst."

"But it isn't done," Cody replied. "Life needs to be rebuilt. Those who were hurt in the flash have a long recovery. Food, medical, water …"

"We don't have that?" she asked.

"Stop," he snapped. "You know what I mean. They're here. They arrived on our soil. Seventeen countries are here."

I spoke up. "But they aren't in Missouri, are they?"

"The chief made contact," Cody said. "They know we're alive. They will sweep the country. It takes time."

"And will they enforce this law you talked about?" I asked.

"What law?" Cody questioned.

Avon clarified, "How soon you forget? The humanitarian violation."

Confidently, Cody nodded. "Yes. Yes, they will. The chief made the report about Silver Bend They will look into it. Justice will be served. It will."

"Not fast enough," I told him.

His eyes shifted from me to Avon. He watched her lift the long bag. "Where are you going?"

"I think you know," Avon said. "We waited long enough."

"Is that ... is that a rifle bag?" Cody asked, then sprang in our way to stop us. "You can't do this. I want her brought to justice as much as you do. What are you going to do? Go to Silver Bend, find her and kill her?"

I shook my head. "In a sense, yes. But she won't know what's coming. Just like my mother didn't see it coming. I thought about looking at her and telling her it was for my mom, but she doesn't deserve that. She preached an eye for an eye. She'll get an eye for an eye."

"So you think it's right to go and avenge your mother's death?" Cody asked.

"I do."

He looked at Avon. "You're an adult. Really? You think this is the best choice?"

"It's what she needs and wants," Avon replied.

"And you're just going to help her?"

"Yes. Al was there for me," Avon said. "If this is what Sofie wants for her mother, then this is what I do."

"That's absurd. Is this what your mother would want you to do?" he asked me. "You think Al would want you to go into this town and Clint Eastwood this Stacey woman?"

"She wanted her dead," I snapped.

"But your mother wouldn't have done it."

"I think she would have," I said calmly. "This is what needs to be done, Cody. My mother's story isn't finished."

"Sofie, I am telling you this is not the way she wants her story to end," he said. "What happened to Al was horrible, wrong, and heartbreaking. Tragic. But it is what it is."

253

"Yeah, you can say that because it isn't your mother." I brushed by him to the door.

"Sofie," he called out. "Avon, please. Just … stay put."

"We'll be back," Avon walked out.

I glanced one last time at Cody and to the pleading look in his eyes. He was a good man. I knew he was affected by what happened to my mom. I watched as he desperately tried to save her.

I just couldn't understand why he would want to save Stacey.

We had talked about it since we buried my mother. Julie was from Silver Bend and was able to tell us where we could just walk in. Which route we could take. It was all planned out.

Maybe subconsciously I waited to implement our plan in hopes I'd change my mind. But I didn't. Each day that passed, each day without my mother, I grew more resentful.

I hid my pain behind my anger.

We took the highway north and eight miles from Silver Bend. A few miles from where we planned to stop the car and walk. Then we saw the truck.

It was a military truck, it moved slowly down the highway in our direction. Painfully slow. Soldiers walked on both sides of the truck and in front.

As we drove closer I saw they weren't our soldiers. The uniforms were different colors of camouflage and the flag patch on their arms looked like a German flag.

I expected them to stop us, question us like some bad war movie, but they didn't. A few of them looked at us as we passed.

They were there to help and not to strong arm. Obviously we didn't need help. So they rolled on by.

Something told me that we could abandon our plan of stopping at Gus' Truck stop and walking the two miles to Silver Bend.

I told Avon to keep driving and she did.

We made it all the way to Silver Bend. No enforcers to stop us, no roadblocks.

Dixie Dips was a restaurant located just outside of the town. Two military trucks were there. They were United States military vehicles, but the soldiers were not.

There were four of them standing by the truck. German soldiers.

It was there we parked Avon's SUV and with the bag slung around her shoulder, we walked into town.

We had one focus.

Find Stacey.

I knew from speaking to Julie that Stacey's base of operations was the bank. Silver Bend wasn't big.

The bank was only a couple blocks away.

As we made our journey I saw only a couple people from Silver Bend. They stood outside a tent with a red cross on it.

"I think that truck we saw was headed to Carthage," Avon said.

"You think?"

"I do. We were wrong. Help *is* in Missouri."

"But are they going to do anything about the likes of Stacey?" I questioned.

"Does it matter?" Avon stopped walking. She slipped the bag from her shoulder, set it on the ground and unzipped it.

I wondered why she did that all of the sudden, then I saw. Not only were we at the bank but Stacey stood out front with two military men.

I froze. My blood felt cold as it ran through my veins. I could feel my own body fighting the rage.

We stepped closer. The military men were speaking to her. It was hard to tell by Stacey's expression what was being said.

Avon raised the rifle holding the scope to her eye level and she aimed. She stepped with determination and without fear toward Stacey.

I could tell she didn't care who was around.

She was delivering justice.

A slight commotion erupted when Avon was spotted. Suddenly, not only the two men with Stacey turned and aimed, but three other soldiers joined in as well.

Stacey shifted her eyes and turned my way.

"You killed my mother," I said calmly. "You killed her."

Stacey didn't respond. She looked shocked.

"Put down the weapon," the one man ordered. "Put it down."

"An eye for an eye," Avon stated.

Stacey took a deep breath and faced us. "It's okay." She waved her hand to the military men then looked at Avon. "Do what you need to do."

"Drop your weapon! Now!" someone ordered.

Looking over, I watched Avon's finger on the trigger. She could do it. I knew it.

"I have her, Sofie," Avon said. "I have her dead in my scope."

I knew at that second that if Avon fired, yes, Stacey would die, but so would Avon.

That wasn't what I wanted.

I hated the woman that stood before me, bold and not afraid to die. I hated her for what she did to my mother.

Eye for an eye.

If I handed justice to Stacey, Avon would be served justice.

Is this what your mother would want you to do?

I heard Cody's voice in my head.

I was holding my breath, and I with puckering lips along with a conscience, I turned to Avon. "Don't do it."

"Are you sure?"

"Don't do it. It's not worth your life."

"I don't care," Avon said. "I don't have a family."

"Yeah, you do. Me."

After a beat, she lowered her weapon and the soldiers rushed our way to apprehend us. They wasted no time taking us into custody as Stacey watched smug.

A part of me thought it was so unfair. She was alive after taking so many lives, killing my mother and we were taken into custody.

I wasn't worried about what would happen to us.

Too much was going on for them to keep us, charge us, or make us pay.

It didn't matter.

In the end, we did the right thing. We held on to our humanity when it slipped away from so many people.

I realized at that moment Cody pleaded with me, not so he could save Stacey, but to save me. He wanted to save me from my own vengeance and anger.

Killing Stacey wouldn't bring my mother back.

He was right. It was not how my mother's story was meant to end.

My mother would want her story to end with me doing the right thing. With me still being alive when the dust of the event settled.

It was a long road to recovery and healing, but for my mother, I would finish her story ... the way she wanted.

ABOUT THE AUTHOR

Jacqueline Druga is a native of Pittsburgh, PA. Her works include genres of all types but she favors post-apocalypse and apocalypse writing.

For updates on new releases you can find the author on:
Facebook: @jacquelinedruga
Twitter: @gojake
www.jacquelinedruga.com